Meet Me
under the
Mistletoe

a holiday romance novella

DANIELLE BAKER

Also by Danielle Baker

Petoskey Stone Series

Love Unbound

Best Kept Secrets

A Heart So Wild

When Hearts Collide

Holiday Romance Novella Collection

Be Mine, Valentine

Birthday Wishes

Meet Me Under the Mistletoe

Coming Soon

Keep watch for the
multi-author collaboration trilogy
SKY RIDGE HOTSHOTS
coming January 2025!
with
Sloane St. James
Paisley Hope
Danielle Baker

Foreword

Please keep in mind that these holiday novellas are written to be fast-paced, quick reads with flash-fire-burn spice. Enjoy, my darlings.

Content/Trigger Warnings
Mention of Parental Death
Bondage/Blindfolding

My Christmas gift to you, book besties! We all need a Theo in our book-boyfriend menagerie.

Chapter One

Noelle

"Yes, I will remember the—"

I sigh, closing my eyes and pinching the bridge of my nose between my thumb and forefinger as my mother continues talking excitedly on the other end of the phone. I have her on speaker so Willow, my little sister, can hear and she rolls her lips in to keep from laughing out loud.

Trying again, I say loudly, "Mom, I know, I will remember to bring it—"

"—*there's just so much to do*. We haven't hosted our Christmas Eve party since your dad passed, and with Beau's surprise, I just want it to be *perfect*—" my mom continues enthusiastically. I sigh again. "Don't forget, Noelle—"

"Mom! I promise, I will not forget the mistletoe. I know that's a huge part of Beau's plan and it would—"

"*Oh my goodness*, I'm just so excited! I've hardly slept a wink since he took me out to dinner to tell me— And Willow—"

Willow waves her hands frantically out in front of her, and I grin slyly as I say excitedly, "Oh yeah, she's right here! Why don't you talk to her!"

Willow glares at me, fire in her hazel eyes as she has no choice but to take the phone from my hand as I shove it at her. I grin widely as Willow says cheerily, "Hey, Mom! Yeah, we are so excited, too—"

Taking the moment of blessed peace, I take a gulp of my coffee—cringing when I realize it has long since gone cold. Tossing the disposable cup and its cold remnants into the garbage, I snag my jacket off the hook by the door and shove my arms through the sleeves.

"Don't you dare leave me—" Willow whisper hisses, holding the phone away from her face, and I grin again as I skip toward the front door of *Three Blossom Haven*, the floral shop myself and my two sisters manage together. Willow taps the screen of my cellphone and mutes the call, hissing to my retreating back, "You better bring me a giant coffee, you traitor! And I'm posting something vile on your Insta!"

Mentally running through all the photos in my phone's library, I shrug and turn at the door, singing, "Worth it!"

Laughing as I exit the flower shop, I make the quick walk

down the snow-covered sidewalk toward *Beau's*, our favorite coffee shop next door. Snow is falling like crazy, blanketing everything in fluffy white flakes. Swinging open the glass door, I shake the snow out of my hair as I cross the polished concrete floor toward the counter and the man that stands behind it.

Beau Collins, his dark hair and beard threaded through with silver, looks up as I approach, and he smiles. A flannel shirt is left unbuttoned over a plain black t-shirt, and the sleeves are rolled up to his elbows, revealing tattooed forearms. My sister's kryptonite.

"You're making my life very difficult, Beau Collins," I grumble, but can't contain the grin, shaking my head as I stop at the counter. His low chuckle makes my smile broaden. "You bastard, you knew exactly what you were doing when you got my mother involved with your plans!"

Bracing his hands on the counter, he leans on them and nods, not an ounce of remorse on his face as he grins. "I love your mother, and I knew that this would make her happy. She deserves that as much as any of you girls."

I scrunch up my face and narrow my eyes on the man that's been making my life hell for the last week. "You better make this the best night of Val's life, because I haven't slept in a week getting ready for this damn party. I left Willow on the phone with my mom and she's threatening to post trash to my social media in retribution."

Beau laughs out loud, straightening and turning to pluck two large disposable coffee cups from a stack on his left. Pouring two coffees—the man doesn't even have to ask at this point, the magical mind reader that he is—tops them with to-go lids, and then slides them across the counter towards me. He looks at me then, a flash of nervousness in his dark brown eyes. "She's going to say yes, right?"

I reach out and cover one of his hands with mine and squeeze lightly. Whispering earnestly, I tell him, "Beau, she would say yes to you a million times."

He nods and takes a deep breath in before exhaling heavily. "Good."

A roar of laughter echoes from the back stock room and my head whips toward the sound. A moment later, a blonde head appears and a wide grin splits his face, phone in his hand as he stares down at it. Theo Collins strides toward me and Beau, the grin growing wider as he gets closer. I narrow my eyes on him.

Theo Collins is both my best friend and the very bane of my existence at the same time. We have a love/hate relationship that has spanned our entire lives, starting way back in kindergarten.

Leaning his hip against the counter, he grins over at me and I narrow my eyes suspiciously again. "What, Theo?"

His lips tip down in a smirk, his blue eyes twinkling mischievously. "Noe, I had no idea you were so desperate for a hook-up."

"What are you talking about?" I snap, pinning him with a stare. His grin just gets wider, and then he turns the phone to show me the screen. My eyes scan the post quickly, mouth dropping open. "*That little twat—*"

Theo laughs harder, nearly wheezing, and he reaches up to swipe at his eyes. "That is some *sexy* lingerie—"

The photo in the post is of me, modeling an absolutely massive pair of women's red satin underwear and a bra that could hold giant beach balls. The set had been a gag gift for my twenty-ninth birthday earlier this year and the underwear could fit nine grown adults in them. I'm fully clothed beneath the gag gift, but still—

"Ohmygod, I'm going to *murder* her—"

Beau chuckles, shaking his head. "She did warn you."

Theo howls with laughter and reads out loud, "*Female, 29, looking for a Christmas date—or just come meet me under the mistletoe. This is the sexiness you can expect—*"

I fairly growl in rage and swipe up the two coffees, turning on my heel. I nearly make it to the door before Theo's voice rings out, "Wait, Noe! Where do I apply?" Staring at the photo harder, he cocks his head to the side in confusion and asks, "Wait, this was your birthday... Why don't I remember this? I was there that night, where the fuck was I when this happened? How did I miss this?!"

Glaring at him over my shoulder, I flip him off, which only makes him laugh harder. Slamming out the door, I stalk down the street to the flower shop. Willow is standing with her arms crossed, one blonde eyebrow raised as I enter.

"You're the absolute worst!" I seethe, though my lips twitch with the need to laugh as I cross the room. Slamming the coffee down on the metal work table, I hiss, "You made your point, I won't leave you alone on the phone with Mom again! Now take it down!"

Willow grins widely, opening the app on my phone and swiping through, deleting the post. Handing it back to me, she grins and sing-songs my words back to me, "Totally worth it."

Chapter Two

Noelle

S till fuming over the revenge post to my Insta account—while doing damage control and fielding DM's from those that had seen it before it was taken down—I'm half tempted to ship Willow off to Timbuktu.

Theo has been relentless.

I shut my phone off two hours ago to escape the texts while grocery shopping—what a nightmare that had been. The store had been in literal chaos, last minute shoppers doing their final grocery runs the day before Christmas Eve.

A box of Shells n Cheese, a bag of frozen, microwavable broccoli, half of a roasted rotisserie chicken, and a discounted loaf of French bread is making up my dinner tonight. The next few days will be hectic and noisy and bittersweet, and I don't have the energy to care about making a more balanced meal.

When Beau had first told me and Willow that he wanted to propose to our sister Val on Christmas Eve, we were ecstatic to help him with the plans... But then he'd had to go and get Mom involved—the damn brown-noser that he is—and the plan for a quiet, intimate Christmas Eve proposal had gone out the window as Mom had announced she was bringing back our traditional Compton/Collins Christmas Eve Party in honor of the two families *officially* joining with the engagement of Beau and Val.

Mom hasn't hosted Christmas Eve since Dad died two years ago. Mom usually makes an appearance at Marnie and Drew Collins' home, at least for a little while, before she heads back home. Before Dad died, the four of them were always together; our mom's had been best friends since grade school and our dad's had joined in during and after college and had been best friends as well. When my dad knew his time was coming, he'd made Beau promise to watch out for all of us—Mom included—and he'd done just that. I know he takes Mom out for dinner dates every week, he's always caught up on whatever trashy tv show Willow is obsessed with, and during college football season, he invites me over for every College Football Saturday, something my dad and I used to do every weekend. He helped us move Val back home when her scummy ex-husband cheated on her and she filed for divorce, and even let her rent out the studio apartment over the coffee shop that he owns—which happened to be directly across the tiny landing from his own studio apartment. Val had decided to try dating after her divorce, and when he'd found out she'd been dumped the night before Valentine's Day earlier this year, he'd gallantly stepped in and offered to take her out for a fake date; a fake date that had turned into much more.

I can't begrudge my sister the happiness she's found—finally—after everything she's gone through in the last two years, but knowing what's coming in the next few days... I need to mentally prepare for it.

My roommate's car isn't in the driveway when I pull in, and no tire tracks mar the perfect white blanket of snow that covers the pavement. That's when I remember her telling me she has a corporate Christmas party she's photographing tonight, and that she'd be out late and not to keep dinner for her. Heh. Guess this whole dinner is just for me.

I'm probably too old to have a roommate, closing in on thirty in a few months, but living alone is *lonely*, and honestly, rent is expensive. It's nice to have help with some of the bills, especially in the last year since we opened *Three Blossom Haven*. Getting it off the ground and rebranded took most of our combined savings. And as I inch closer to that big three-oh, I realize I'm probably just destined to being single forever. Dating is stupid, anyway.

Lugging my groceries out of the passenger seat, I step through the six-inch-deep snow in the driveway to the front door. I should shovel a pathway, at least. Belle must have left the porch light on before she left, and I grimace at the Christmas wreath hanging lopsided on the front door.

Belle—my roommate—and I, had put up the janky looking dollar store wreath with glitter holly berries that are half falling off on the front door, and then lined the front windows with strings of multi colored Christmas lights. I have a string of them along the headboard in my bedroom, too, though the rest of them never made it up. Instead, they're piled in a cardboard box in the living room, still in a jumbled, tangled mess. A tiny, tabletop tree sits on one end table in the corner, and a few hastily wrapped gifts sit in front of it.

Normally I go all out for Christmas; my apartment would look like the Christmas aisle of *Hobby Lobby* had thrown up everywhere, with a giant balsam fir, vintage glass icicle ornaments that used to belong to my Nan, three different sizes of white twinkle lights, and Christmas themed décor scattered across every possible surface. I'd once wrapped all the upper cabinet doors in wrapping paper and bows. It had turned out fantastic. Mom had been furious. Dad thought it was hilarious.

It's different without Dad though. No record player dusted off and playing all of his old Christmas records; *The Carpenters Christmas, Osmond Christmas, Elmo & Patsy...* This year, I fully identify with "Percy the Puny Poinsettia".

I sigh heavily, setting my grocery bag on the kitchen counter, devoid of any holiday décor, and empty the contents of the bag. I fill a pot with water and set it to start boiling, and put the broccoli in the microwave to steam.

Sliding my phone out of my pocket, I groan and grimace, powering it back on.

Within seconds of it powering on fully, a barrage of texts and DM's from my Insta account come through, the majority of them from Theo.

Theo

> I think I need an in-person demonstration of that lingerie, in order to make a fully educated decision on whether to take you up on that Christmas date ad.

> Hold on, this calls for corny pick-up lines.

I groan again, shaking my head as I read down the line of

suggestive texts.

Theo

> I'm not Santa, but do you want to sit on my lap and tell me what you want for Christmas?

> Do you like the song "Jingle Bells"? Because I'd like you to jingle my bells.

> We could make this a not-so-silent night.

> Screw the Nice List. Let's both be Naughty and save Santa the trip.

I choke back my laughter at the horribly cheesy pick-up lines and type up a response.

Me

> All you're going to get for Christmas is a harassment charge and a restraining order, you idiot.

The three text bubbles immediately pop up, as if he was waiting for me to respond, and I laugh out loud. I pour the pasta shells into the boiling water on the stove and stir it as my phone pings with another message.

Theo

> **Noe, you wound me. I'll find better ones.**

> **Hold, please.**

I can't help the smile. Theo may be a giant pain in my ass, but he's the best friend I've got—other than Belle—or my sisters. He never fails to make me laugh, even when I don't want to. Val calls us a 'reverse-grumpy-sunshine', something I'm assuming comes from the copious amounts of romance books she's always reading. The text bubbles come back, then disappear. He starts a message several times before deleting it and starting over. Good god, this is going to be a bad one.

Theo

> **If a big man puts you in a bag tomorrow night, don't worry. I told Santa I wanted you for Christmas.**

A snort of laughter escapes me as I stir the pasta. The microwave dings and I hot-potato the steaming hot bag out with the tips of my fingers grasped around one tip of a corner. I place it in the sink and come back to my phone.

Me

> Going for kidnapping charges now lol. I'd rethink this plan, Theo. Orange really isn't your color, Bud.

The text bubbles are back instantly.

Theo

> All I want for Christmas is you, Noe.

> *Christmas Mariah Carey GIF*

New text bubbles appear before I'm finished reading.

> I'll meet you under the mistletoe.

Me

> You're an idiot, Theo.

> Want to come over and watch Home Alone? I have hot chocolate bombs and junk food.

Theo

> Sold. Be there in ten.

I can hear the sound of snow crunching beneath tires as he pulls in ten minutes later. I changed out of my work clothes and put on a comfy, fuzzy pair of light blue pajama pants covered in white snowflakes. A long-sleeved white shirt covers clear up to my neck and the long sleeves are about four inches too long, dangling past my fingertips. I don't have a bra on, but the material is thick enough I'm not altogether worried about it—not that my boobs are large or anything to look at by any stretch of the imagination. Willow was blessed with those while I'd been a chair member of the itty-bitty-titty-committee all my life, though with a good push-up bra, they could look damn good. If I did say so myself.

He doesn't bother knocking, just lets himself in like he owns the place, kicking snow off his boots before toeing them off at the door. He's tall and thin, built like a basketball player—an ode to his high school basketball days.

He's wearing a pair of blue flannel pajama pants, a simple Carhart long sleeved shirt in a dark navy color that compliments his blue eyes, and his usual quilted gray vest, though he strips that down his arms and tosses it over the back of one of the stools at the kitchen counter. He tosses his ballcap down onto the counter and makes his way into the living room, stopping in front of the corner of the couch I've folded myself into, my plate of steaming Shells n Cheese, strips of the rotisserie chicken, broccoli, and a ginormous slice of buttered French bread sitting in my lap. It might not be the most nutritious meal I've had this week, but it's delicious, so I don't care.

"Any of that left? I'm starving." Apparently, Theo doesn't mind a carb overloaded junk meal either.

"On the stove," I mumble around a bite of cheesy pasta, reaching over to hit play on the remote, *Home Alone* already queued up on the tv across the room. "Hot chocolate bombs are in the cupboard, but if you want a beer, there's some in the fridge."

"Which do you want?" he calls from the open fridge.

"Umm. Beer, please."

He's back moments later, a plate of food in one hand and his long, tapered fingers of his other hand wrapped around the necks of two bottles of beer. A lime wedge is shoved halfway into the mouth of mine, and I smile in thanks. He knows me so well it's uncanny sometimes.

He sinks into the opposite corner of the couch and immediately digs into the plate of food in his hand as Kevin McCallister jumps around screaming *'I'm living alone!'* on the tv.

He stretches out his legs in front of him, propping his socked heels on the coffee table. I have a cinnamon scented candle lit in the center of it. The room is dark except for the glow of the tv and the few strings of Christmas lights taped up around the living room windows. I glance over at him, where he's digging into the plate of food balanced in his hand.

His dark blonde hair is flattened slightly from his hat, and he reaches up a hand to run it through the boyishly long strands, ruffling it and fluffing it as if sensing my scrutiny. The sleeves of his long-sleeved navy-blue shirt are pushed up his forearms, and as he moves the muscles bunch and flex.

Theo's unfairly attractive in that goofy 'golden boy next door' sort of way. All long limbs and that easy, lopsided grin that's almost permanently etched on his face. His teeth are straight and white—thanks to the same orthodontist I'd had to go to as a teenager to fix the gap between my two front teeth—though I doubt he still has to wear his stupid retainer every night like I do. His blue eyes are that striking light blue with darker rings around the edges. Where his brother Beau is all dark haired, dark eyed, and grumpy, Theo is the polar opposite.

"Are you ready for tomorrow?"

I sigh and shrug. "Yes and no. I'm excited for Beau and Val. Exhausted from work and trying to plan this whole party with less than two weeks' notice and keep it a secret from Val." I shrug again. "I miss my dad."

"I know you do." I glance up at him. He winks. "He'd be

happy that our families are finally *family*. And he'd be proud of what you girls have accomplished. You know that, right?"

"I know," I whisper, fighting the sting in my nose as tears burn my eyes. "Christmases are just tough. This feels weird, going back to a tradition without him being here for it." I shift in my corner of the couch. "How excited are your parents for the engagement?"

He laughs out loud, raising his blonde brows and grinning. "My mom is beside herself. When she found out they were dating she cried. *Cried,* Noelle. She blubbered on about how she'd never thought Beau would give her a daughter-in-law, and for it to be Val? She's over the damn moon. She loves you three more than she loves Beau and me."

"That is so not even true," I laugh, shaking my head and slapping his bicep with the back of my hand, ignoring the hardness of the muscle beneath the material of his shirt or the way a zing races up my fingers at the contact. "She was so mad at me that one year I licked all the Christmas cookies so no one else could have any. I don't think she's ever forgiven me for that."

"I think watching you eat them until you were sick was payment enough," he chuckled.

"I still can't look at a gingerbread cookie." I grimace at the memory of the stomachache I'd had after eating almost a full tray of the damn things.

Theo polishes off his plate and leans forward, setting it on the coffee table, before leaning back into the corner of the couch. Resting one arm along the back cushions, he angles his body so that he can lift his legs and feet onto the couch lengthwise. I shift, raising my plate so he can place his feet in my lap. He's so damn tall he takes up the whole couch, the big oaf.

"You're lucky your feet don't stink," I mutter, lowering my plate back down so that it hovers over his ankles. He chuckles, wiggling his socked toes. I'm full, but it's so delicious I don't want to stop eating. Sighing, I take one more bite of the cheesy pasta and set my fork down on the plate, then set the plate aside on the end table next to me. I take a long swallow of my beer, emptying it, then heave myself to my feet, forcing him to pull his legs back enough to allow me up.

I pick up both of our plates and take them to the kitchen, setting them in the sink. "Do you want another beer?"

"Sure, thanks."

I'm back and sinking into the corner of the couch again a few moments later, passing him his beer, and he replaces his feet in my lap. I'm mostly turned to face him now, my back resting against the armrest. I prop my elbow on the back cushion and lean my cheek into my palm, my eyes on the tv.

"What did you ask Santa for Christmas?"

I side-eye him and sigh. "Nothing exciting, if that's what you're asking."

He shifts in his corner of the couch. "I mean it. There's got to be something you want, right?"

I shrug. "Sure. All my bills paid, new winter tires for my car, *the moon and all the stars...*" He glares at me and I roll my eyes. I know what he means. "I don't know, Theo. If I want or need something, I usually just get it myself. One of the perks of being a grown up with grown up money." I glance over at him. "What about you?"

He shrugs, the same way I did, and stretches his legs out. His heels are in the valley that my criss-crossed legs have created. He smiles, a small half grin that doesn't quite reach his eyes. "Santa can't bring me what I want."

I turn my head to look at him fully, though I don't say anything.

"No witty response?" he teases, his blue eyes regaining some of their twinkle. Maybe it had just been the lighting.

"I doubt Santa is allowed to deliver illegal substances or hookers, Theo."

He laughs out loud, letting his head tip back slightly. "There it is."

I grin back, then return my attention to the tv. We're quiet for a time, and I nestle deeper into the couch. Harry and Marv are trying to find their way into the McCallister house, and I can't help the chuckle that escapes me.

"Are you bringing a date tomorrow?"

My head is resting against the cushion and I raise it, swinging my head over to look at him with a baleful glower. "Don't start on that stupid post, Theo."

"But are you?" he asks again, his chin resting in the palm of his hand, his elbow on the arm rest. The blue of his stare is unnerving in intensity.

"No?" I scoff, rolling my eyes. "Why would I want to bring a date to our joint family Christmas chaos? I'm not trying to impress anyone, and I don't want to take any of the attention away from Beau and Val." My eyes widen slightly. "Why? Are *you* bringing a date?"

His lips tip down just a touch at the corners, a barely noticeable shrug lifting one shoulder. "No."

"Is there anyone you would ask?" I nudge, grinning lightly. A full belly and the contents of these beers have taken all the tension out of my shoulders. And teasing Theo is one of my

23

favorite past times.

Again, he shrugs lightly, lifting his beer to his lips. My eyes track the movement, and I can feel his gaze on my face. When he swallows and lowers the beer bottle back to his lap, he says, "She's...not interested."

"*Ooooh,*" I murmur quietly, teasing. "So, there *is* someone that Theo Collins has his eye on. What kind of idiot wouldn't be interested? Wait. It's because she's actually got a brain, right?"

He glares over at me, and I laugh before placing my palm over his shin, squeezing lightly. His muscles jump beneath my fingers, and I can't stop the instant pitter patter of my heart in my chest. *What the fuck? What is wrong with me?* And why am I even the slightest bit jealous that Theo has feelings for someone? I don't even like Theo. Not like that.

Right?

"The timing isn't right, is all," he finally answers, his blue eyes still trained on mine. "She'll come around."

I lower my brows over my eyes. "You're not stalking this woman, right? We're not adding stalking to harassment and kidnapping, Theo."

He laughs out loud, shaking his head. "Stalking is a bit extreme. I prefer... opportunistic."

"Theo..."

He rolls his eyes and grins boyishly. "Orange isn't my color, remember?"

Chapter Three

Theo

Her head is tipped against the cushion, cheek pressed into the soft material, eyes closed. The movie ended a while ago, but I remain where I am, content to watch her as she sleeps. I'd convinced her to shift sideways and stretch her legs out, so that our legs are parallel to each other and sort of twisted together like a pretzel. I'd also pulled the blanket off the back of the couch and draped it over the both of us, and her fingers are fisted in it, holding the softness beneath her chin. Which I'm glad for, to be honest, because watching her all night with her fucking nipples poking through the material of her shirt was both a blessed gift and pure torture.

I've loved Noelle Compton since I was a kid.

Not that she's ever known how I feel about her.

I'm just that goofy guy that's always been there. The one that will always make her laugh, piss her off, sit and watch a silly Christmas movie because I know it's her favorite... Take her to prom when her douchebag of a date ditched her, even though I was on crutches from a stupid soccer injury.

Or hold her while she cried when her dad died. God, the memory of the grief that had poured out of her...it still punches me in the gut. I hate seeing her upset—though admittedly, pissing her off is one of this life's finer things.

I know the next couple days are going to be tough for her, for all of us. Hank Compton was a wonderful dad and husband, a great mentor, and the best friend my dad had ever had. Beau had always been a tag-along with our dads, but I'd been so involved in sports—if for no other reason than to keep myself busy so I wouldn't obsessively think about Noelle—that I hadn't spent as much time with our dads as Beau had.

I was the class clown, the troublemaker; and all of it was to try and get Noelle's attention.

It worked, just not in the way my underdeveloped teenage brain had hoped. She saw me as the lovable idiot that was more like a brother than anything. Now, at almost thirty, that seems to be all she's ever going to see me as.

I don't want her to see me like a damn brother, though. Or, much worse, as her *golden retriever bestie*. I roll my eyes and let out a self-deprecating scoff. What a way to be known by the woman I've loved and wanted my entire life. A fucking dog begging for any scrap of attention. *Woof.*

She lets out a soft snore and I grin, continuing to watch her as she sleeps. Her roommate, Belle—short for Annabelle, though I'd learned she hates being called that—came home earlier, setting a heavy looking camera bag down by the door. She'd disappeared into her room a while ago. The door squeaks open now and I turn my head, nodding to the woman as she steps out wearing flannel pjs and a hoodie that looks like it's three sizes too big. She pads over to the couch and shakes her head, smiling slightly.

"Are you going to wake her up or just leave her on the couch?" she asks on a whisper.

I turn my attention back to Noelle and purse my lips. "I might carry her to bed. She's going to get a crick in her neck sleeping like that."

She pats my shoulder as she moves away toward the kitchen, and I hear a cupboard open and then the kitchen faucet running. She carries her glass of water with her back to the bedroom and says a quiet, "Good night, Theo."

"Night," I murmur back, turning my attention back to Noelle. I shift so that I can leverage myself up off the couch, trying not to jostle her and wake her, but she's out hard and doesn't stir. I stretch my spine for a moment and then bend over her, sliding my arms under her knees and beneath her back. I lift her and the blanket together, knowing full well I'm never going to get it loose from the fists she has it clutched in beneath her chin. Her head lolls onto my shoulder as I get her situated in my arms, and then I'm crossing the living room to the bedroom I know is hers. I push the door open and step inside.

A string of colorful Christmas lights is strung up along the top edge of her headboard, filling the room with a warm glow, just enough for me to see where I'm going. I lay her down on the mattress and tuck her in as gently as I can, covering her with the blanket again and pulling the comforter over her. She snuggles into the pillow and lets out a sigh, her eyes never opening.

I know I should back away, turn myself and leave her room, but my feet are like lead, keeping me planted where I am as I stare down at her, half braced over her by my arms. My traitorous hand moves of its own accord and my eyes track the movement. I draw my fingers through her dark hair, sweeping it away from her face. She's facing me, though part of her is bathed in shadows, part of her highlighted by the Christmas lights from above her.

Her mouth is parted slightly, those dusty rose-colored lips I've wanted to taste for so long soft and malleable. I let my thumb sweep over her cheekbone and then down to her lips, brushing softly. Her breathing never changes, and my dick is getting hard just being this close to her. Dammit she's so beautiful.

Leaning down, I press my lips to her temple, right at her hairline, letting myself linger there for longer than I should. She smells like flowers, roses and jasmine and something earthier, maybe cedar.

Fuck, I need to go. I kiss her temple once more and whisper, "Good night, Angel."

And then I straighten, ignoring the ache in my dick, to let myself out as silently as I can.

Chapter Four

Noelle

As soon as the door clicks shut, my eyes snap open and I let out the shaky, panting breaths I'd tried so damn hard to keep steady. I can hear him out in the living room, the shuffle of his feet on the floor as he moves around—probably blowing out the candle I'd carelessly left burning—turning off the tv, taking care of our empty beers. The rasp of his vest being zipped, and then the quiet snick as the front door is shut behind him, followed by the thud of a car door shutting, and the rumble of the engine starting.

He'd carried me to bed, tucked me in, and I'd only woken as his gentle, sweeping touch grazed my cheek... my lips. It had taken all of my concentration not to react with a gasp at the electricity that had zapped through me at the contact of his finger against my mouth. And then he'd kissed my head, not once, but twice. The feel of his lips against my hair had made me realize maybe I wanted to feel those lips on other places, too.

But it was the whisper quiet "*Good night, Angel*" that had nearly done me in. I was sure he'd known I was awake. I wasn't *that* good of an actress. The gentle huskiness of his voice, the intensity and longing in that voice that I had heard in all its forms over the course of our lives...but this. This was a new side of Theo I'd never seen, or maybe just hadn't ever noticed. Maybe a side of Theo he never let anyone see at all.

His words came back to me from earlier, then. "*She's not interested*" and "*The timing isn't right is all. She'll come around*" reverberated in my head.

He's not talking about me, right?

Right?!

I'm wide awake now, lying flat on my back in bed. Staring up at the ceiling, the Christmas lights strung up on my headboard casting a colorful light show above me. But all I can think about is Theo's lips, how his finger had brushed my own mouth. Now my whole body is on fire.

Throwing off the comforter and the blanket, I sit straight up in bed. There's no way I'm falling back to sleep anytime soon. *Dammit, Theo!*

Padding out to the kitchen, I grab a glass of water and drink half of it, standing at the kitchen sink. I was right earlier, he had blown out that candle I left burning, turned off the TV, and the even locked the door on his way out.

The little window over the sink faces out toward the road. It's dark out, but the light post across the street casts a glow on the ground below. It's snowing, the big, fat kind of snowflakes that cover everything in a thick layer of snow after just a short time. The kind that if you catch them, they're the pretty snowflakes, with the perfectly imperfect, symmetrical points.

Theo's footprints and the tire tracks from his car are almost covered already, even though he left less than ten minutes ago. I groan. My car is going to be buried by morning.

Dragging myself back to bed, I slide beneath the covers and snag the tv remote off the bedside table. The TV across the room comes on, and I queue up Will Farrell's ELF in the hopes that it will lull me back to sleep.

Chapter Five

Noelle

My late night of Christmas movies is biting me in the ass this morning. I never set my alarm last night before falling asleep, so I got the pleasure of waking up to a dozen missed calls and text messages—each one getting more threatening than the last—from my sisters, who have been at *Three Blossom Haven* since dawn. Oops.

So I'm headed into *Beau's* to get a vat of 'Forgive Me For Over-Sleeping' coffee to offer up to Val and Willow so they don't use me as a sacrifice to Krampus later.

Theo is standing behind the counter when I push through the glass door, the full panes frosted over with ice from the cold outside. The snow is still coming down in heavy, fat flakes. The city's snow removal team is out in full force, clearing the streets and sidewalks, but it's really no use; the snow is coming down so fast the roads and sidewalks are covered back up with the white fluff almost immediately.

Despite *his* late night, he looks well rested, his usual grin in place, blue eyes dancing. Instead of his typical backwards ball cap on his head, he's sporting a faux fur lined Santa hat, the white ball on the end trailing close to his shoulder. A muted red, long-sleeved t-shirt is stretched across his chest, three check boxes with Naughty, Nice, and Tried My Best in bold white lettering. The check is slashed through the Tried My Best option, and I can't help but roll my eyes as I step up closer to the counter. His grin gets wider.

"What? You don't like it?" he asks, gesturing down to his chest.

"Oh no, it suits you perfectly," I laugh, shaking my head. "Santa might skip over you tonight anyway."

"I doubt that," he mutters, grinning. He winks. "What can I do for you? No, wait, *what can I do you for*? Ah shit, I mean, *can I do you*?"

"Theo Collins, you better go wash that mouth out with soap and apologize to Miss Compton—"

Theo laughs out loud, winking at me again as he turns to our second-grade teacher, Mrs. Greene. "I promise you, it's not what it sounds like—"

"Oh, I think I want to hear this apology, Theo," I say with all the seriousness I can muster. My lips twitch. He glares at me out of the corner of his eyes, and I roll my lips in between my teeth to keep from laughing, too. "You have been awfully naughty lately."

He glares at me for a heartbeat longer before grinning winningly over at our old teacher. "Mrs. Greene, I'm sorry you had to hear that. Noelle, I'm sorry for my depravity. I'll do better." When Mrs. Greene finally nods and shuffles away with her cappuccino, Theo braces himself on his hands on the counter, leaning over it toward me. He winks, then lets those blue eyes travel down to my mouth before raising them slowly to look me in the eyes again. This stare is intense and heated. It makes my breath stutter and my heart pound in my throat. "You have no idea just how *naughty* I can be, Angel."

Oh.

Those butterflies are back, wreaking havoc on my insides. He's so close, if I just leaned forward the slightest bit, our noses would touch. And if our noses touched, it wouldn't be that far off to tilt our heads just the tiniest bit until our mouths did, too—

Yanking myself back half a step, I suck in a much-needed lungful of air. My eyes are bouncing between his, my brain not fully processing where my own thoughts had taken me. What the shit is my brain even doing?

He licks his lips, dropping his eyes to my mouth once

more, before pulling himself upright behind the counter, putting necessary space between us again. "So, what can I get for you this morning?"

"Umm. Coffee," I stutter lamely, then wish I could slam my head into the nearest wall when he grins slyly, as if he knows just how much he's rattled me. The asshole. I shake my head and straighten my shoulders. "Coffees for Willow and Val and myself, please. Big ones. I overslept and they're threatening to offer me up as a sacrifice to Krampus."

"Well, we can't have that," Theo chuckles, tapping on the large touch screen in front of him. The cashier till dings and slides open, and he closes it swiftly. "Beau says anything you girls get today is on the house."

"Thank you," I whisper, dropping my purse at my side. I still stuff a twenty into the tip jar just because. He glowers at me, but I just shrug. "Is he nervous?"

"He's in the back room compulsively cleaning and organizing the stock racks," he says, chuckling as he begins making our coffees. "We had a rush about an hour ago but we're in a lull, and once that hit, he was back to panicking. We'll get another rush in a bit; it'll take his mind off of it for a little while. I'm glad we're closing early, I'm not sure I can handle a whole day of him losing his mind."

"You know what, when you finally get around to finding some woman that you want to propose to, I'm going to remember this," Beau grumbles as he stalks out of the back room, a large box of cups and lids in his arms. He sets it down on the counter beside them and starts unloading the contents. "And I'll give you as much shit as you've given me in the last two weeks."

"Maybe if he got around to asking his *mystery girl* on a date—"

"Mystery girl?" Beau asks, turning to Theo, who has his back to us as he tops the three coffee drinks with whipped cream and green and red sprinkles. "What mystery girl?"

"I don't have a mystery girl," Theo snaps over his shoulder at his brother. I grin over at Beau. Theo spins toward me, pointing one finger at my chest. "And that was a private conversation, you traitor."

"So there *is* a mystery girl." Beau grins, too, folding his heavily tattooed arms across his chest. He isn't decked out in Christmas gear like Theo, though he does have a red, white, and black flannel pulled on over his usual black t-shirt. The sleeves are pushed to his elbows, and he has on a pair of faded, well-worn black jeans. His dark hair that's threaded through with silver is worn longer than traditional, falling over his brow and curling slightly at the nape of his neck.

Willow once told us he reminded her of Skeet Ulrich, and I haven't been able to un-see it since.

Theo turns toward me, coffee carrier loaded down with the three decked out coffees in three of the spots, a handful of wrapped, house made chocolate biscotti standing straight up in the last. I wiggle my fingers together in front of me in excitement. That will definitely get me out of the Krampus Sacrifice. Hopefully, anyway.

He snatches the carrier back before I can grab hold of it, though. He glowers at me. "You owe me."

"Yes, yes, whatever you want," I mutter, waggling my fingers outward, silently asking for the carrier.

"That's a dangerous promise," Theo murmurs quietly, setting the carrier in my outstretched hands. My fingers brush across the backs of his as I take hold of it, and the electricity that zaps through me has nothing to do with static cling. I swallow hard, my eyes shooting up to his. "I will be collecting on that, Noelle."

Chapter Six

Noelle

"I'm sorry, I'm sorry! But I come bearing Christmas coffees—*with sprinkles*—and chocolate biscotti!"

I plunk the drink carrier down in the center of the stainless-steel work table in the back room of *Three Blossom Haven*, between Val and Willow. Val is glaring daggers at me, but Willow is just grinning as she plucks her coffee out of the carrier and snags a biscotti.

"Told you the Krampus thing would work," she mumbles to Val out of the corner of her mouth as she unwraps the biscotti, and Val rolls her eyes.

Val points the heavy-duty floral shears in her hand at me, waggling them ominously. "You're lucky it's Christmas and I'm feeling generous today. And that Theo is always saving your ass."

"Hey! He is *not* always saving my ass—"

"What about last week when he went out of his way to go over to your house to pick up and bring you your *shoes* because your dumb ass came into work in your *slippers*? And then went out and bought you a brand-new pair of slippers because you ruined the pair you were wearing in the snow—"

"Or what about three days ago when you locked yourself out of your house and he came over with his key to let you in at two in the morning? You never did tell us why you were out that late on a Wednesday, by the way—"

"And how about last summer when your car broke down on your way to Traverse City to pick up Mom from the airport and he dropped everything he was doing to come get you, fixed your car, and picked up Mom?" Willow lifts her coffee to her lips to take a sip, raising her eyebrows high and staring at her over the lid of the cup. "He's like your own personal Knight in Cozy Flannel."

"He doesn't wear flannels all the time—"

"He and Beau should buy stock in some flannel shirt company. They're always in flannels," Val mutters and rolls her eyes again. "It's like the man doesn't know that other shirts exist. Half of his closet is different colored flannel shirts, the other half is plain black or white t-shirts, and he's got a handful of dark or black jeans. That's all the man wears!"

"But that's Beau, Theo doesn't wear them that often—" I protest, but honestly, they're both right.

"Theo always has on some kind of off the wall or inappropriate graphic tee under his," Willow laughs, taking a bite of the biscotti. She hums in approval, doing a little shimmy of appreciation of the deliciousness. "Last week he had on a t-shirt that said 'Deez Nuts Roasting Co'. I thought Beau was going to have an aneurysm when he saw it. But yes, he always has one on. Or that gray quilted vest."

"That he *does* wear all the time during the winter," I admit with a chuckle.

"No, he starts wearing that in September and wears it through to April," Val laughs, shaking her head. "Pretty sure Marnie buys him a new one every Christmas."

"So he knows what he likes, and he knows he looks good in it," I mumble around a gulp of my coffee. I lick the sugary sprinkles off my top lip.

"Oh, he looks good in it, huh?" Willow asks, raising her eyebrows again.

"Oh, come on, just because we've known them forever and they're practically family doesn't mean we can't admit that they're both stupidly hot—" I turn to Val, gesturing wildly with my hands, something I do when I'm nervous and can't stop the word vomit. "I mean seriously, Val, you shacked up with Beau, not that I blame you one bit, that man is fine with a capital F—"

"Do you want to shack up with Theo?" Willow asks, bracing her hands on the work table, leaning forward excitedly. "I knew it!"

"*No!*" I practically shout, my face heating. I mean, I never thought about it *until last night*, but ever since then it's all that I've been able to think about. Not that they need to know that. "I do however, have eyeballs and a healthy sexual appetite. I'm comfortable enough to admit that Theo's hot as shit."

Willow's face scrunches up in disgust and I can't help but laugh. She gags theatrically. "I don't want to hear about your sexual appetite. We might be close but that's TMI. And no, it's not because I'm a prude. I just don't want to hear about my sisters and their sex lives."

"Is that why you never share details about you and Luck—"

"You sure you don't want to hear about that thing that Beau does with his tongue—"

Val and I start talking at the same time, and Willow claps her hands over her ears, singing a loud chorus of, "*Lalalalalala!*" which makes us both double over with laughter. She drags her hands down and glares at us both. "No, I don't want to talk about what Reeve and I do, nor do I want to hear anything about Beau or *what he does with his tongue!*"

Val and I share a look, grinning widely. "You sure? You could have Luck try it—"

Willow bristles angrily, glaring at first myself, then Val, crossing her arms over her chest. "For your information, you nosy asses, Reeve does amazing things with his tongue, not that it's any of your business!"

Val, having just taken a drink of her coffee, chokes, spitting it out all over the tabletop. I thump her on the back as I shake my head. "Well, that's good."

Val reaches for a handful of paper towels, cleaning up her mess as Willow throws me an aggravated look. "You guys are the worst."

"Yes, but you love us anyway," I tease, winking.

"Can we just get back to work, please?" Willow snaps, throwing her hands up. "Last I checked, my sex life is *the least* interesting topic today—"

Panicking, my instinct is to throw out an elbow, connecting hard with Willow's ribs and she grunts, but at least the words tumbling out of her mouth stop. Thank God Val's back is to us as she takes out a bundle of deep red Dahlias and pearly white Lilies from the commercial cooler across from us. She turns back to the table and spreads them out in front of her.

She blows out a breath and tosses her shoulder length brown hair away from her face as she looks up at us. I lunge for my coffee and take a huge gulp, coughing as it goes down the wrong tube.

"Alright, Willow's right, we need to get these orders out so we can close early. Mom is probably losing her mind at the house trying to get everything done without us there to help," Val says, picking up the floral shears again and snapping them twice—her version of a cook clicking tongs—and blows out another heavy exhale. "Let's focus, girls. Only a few more hours and then we're off for four days!"

"Halleluiah!" Crisis averted.

Chapter Seven

Theo

I might stare a little too long as Noelle walks out the front door of the coffee shop, drink carrier in hand. I might let my gaze follow her down the sidewalk, watch as she tilts her face up to the heavy snow as she walks away.

And then she sticks her tongue out, as if to try and catch one of those fat flakes, and the eroticism of it goes straight to my dick. I almost drop the bottle of water in my hands, my entire system shutting down and going absolutely haywire.

That. *That's* what I want for Christmas. I want her, mouth open, looking up at *me* like she's waiting for what *I* can put on that tongue—

"You're drooling."

Noelle disappears beyond the view of the wide windows along the front of the coffee shop and I find that I can somehow breathe slightly easier. I glare over at Beau, who's leaning up against the back counter, ankles crossed, his muscled arms crossed over his chest. Tattoos cover his forearms, visible from the elbow down. He's staring at me with a shit-eating grin on that stupid face.

"Fuck off."

He tilts his head to one side, that grin widening. "This conversation feels oddly like déjà vu, doesn't it?" He snaps his fingers as if remembering something. "Wait, say it again. I got it, now."

I roll my eyes, heaving a heavy sigh. "Fuck off, Beau."

"No can do, baby brother."

I can't help but laugh. This is *exactly* the conversation we had earlier this year, when Beau had gone and fallen head over heels in love with Val after their fake Valentine's Day date. The world certainly has a way of coming back around to kick people right in the ball sack—

"Have you finally grown a pair large enough to ask her out?"

"*Dude*—" I snap, glancing around the coffee shop. It doesn't seem like anyone heard him, but fuck... "It's not like that with us, okay? Just leave it alone. We're friends."

"Sure, friends that want to boink."

The stare I send his way only makes him chuckle, shifting on his feet. I shake my head, throwing my hands up. "You don't need to fire me, I quit—" Letting my head drop back so that

I'm staring up at the black ceiling tiles above me, I mutter, "Did you really just say *boink*? Good God, Val's made you soft in your old age."

The humor leaves Beau's face as he levels me with a hard stare. "Good thing Val knows there's nothing *soft* about me when she's around—"

"Jesus, you horndog, that's not even what I meant," I mumble, turning back toward the counter. I pick up my long-forgotten coffee, taking a sip. It's lukewarm at best. I toss it down the sink to my left and pour another cup of fresh brew. "But it's good to hear she's not crying anymore. You must have figured something out—"

I know the swipe of his arm is coming and I dodge it with a boom of laughter. His dark eyes are narrowed on me, his stance poised to strike. He might outweigh me in bulk and muscle by thirty pounds, but I'm taller than him by a good four inches, and a helluva lot quicker.

"You watch that mouth when you talk about my wife." Beau's voice is low, deep, and calm, but the undercurrent of possessive rage is there. *Oof. The man has it bad.*

I grin then, straightening. "You called her your wife."

Beau straightens too, his face softening slightly as he tilts his head in thought. He scoffs, shaking his head. "I did, didn't

I?" He reaches up and scrubs one hand across the back of his neck. "I honestly haven't thought about her any other way in months, once I decided I was going to do it... Calling her my girlfriend just feels so... unexceptional, like it doesn't explain how fucking perfect she is for me, or how much she means to me. Fiancé doesn't even feel like enough. I want the world to know that she belongs to me, and that I belong to her. Irrefutably."

I clap him on the back, squeezing his shoulder. "That needs to be in your proposal, or your vows, brother. That was damn moving."

He shoves me away, but his grin is back in place. "Do me a favor? Don't let Noelle forget the mistletoe tonight."

"She won't forget the mistletoe. She's got this." I clap him on the back again. "She knows how important this is, man. We've all got your back tonight. Even if Val says no."

I don't manage to dodge the arm that bands around my neck this time, my laughter silenced by his forearm as he holds me in a loose chokehold. Admittedly, I probably deserve this one.

Chapter Eight

Noelle

Worst sister award goes to: Me.

I forgot the mistletoe.

The. Mistletoe.

The one big, pivotal piece to Beau's Christmas Eve proposal. I forgot it. Just like Mom knew I would. *Shiiitttt.*

Left it hiding behind a massive Christmas Poinsettia, carefully wrapped and ready to take with me when we'd locked up. I was supposed to grab it and stuff it into the pocket of my jacket when Val wasn't looking. But it was like she was *everywhere*, and I didn't have the chance without her seeing me, and then we left, and I forgot it.

"Fuck. Fuck fuck fuck."

"Goose."

Spinning, I glare over at Willow. "*Not funny*. I need you to distract Mom and Val and Beau."

Her eyes narrow on me. "What did you do?"

Licking my lips, I mumble, "I forgot the mistletoe."

"I'm sorry, I didn't catch that—"

"*I forgot the mistletoe at the shop!*" I whisper hiss through clenched teeth, glancing at the doorway that leads from the living room into the kitchen, where Val and Beau and our mother are working on the final touches for dinner. Beau and Theo's parents should be here any second, so that will work as a distraction to my sudden absence...

"You're so dead," Willow laughs, shaking her head.

"Shut up," I mumble, pressing my fingers to my temples in an effort to stave off the headache I can feel forming. "I can fix this. I can sneak out and be back before they even realize I left—"

A knock at the front door is my saving grace. Bolting forward, I shout, "I've got it!"

Swinging the door open, my smile falls. "Oh, it's just you."

Luck, Willow's boyfriend, just smirks. "Uh, nice to see you, too, Noelle."

Willow pushes me aside and Luck steps in over the threshold to close the door, then leans down to kiss her. "Merry Christmas, Goldie."

"Merry Christmas," my sister whispers against his lips and I fake a dramatic gag. She glares at me from around his bicep.

She pushes Luck toward the kitchen. "Mom, Val, and Beau are in the kitchen. Give me just a second with my sister—"

His deep, rumbling chuckle echoes down the hall as he grins over at me before walking away. Willow spins to face me and opens her mouth.

Another knock on the front door has me spinning in place and yanking the door open. My smile this time is genuine as Marnie and Drew Collins say in unison, "Merry Christmas!" Ushering them inside, I'm pulled into tight hugs by both of them. Marnie smells like cookies and vanilla. She's one of those 'everyone's auntie' moms that everyone in the world should have the fortune of having at some point in their lives.

Drew Collins is the epitome of the 'guys guy' dad. Summertime the man could only be seen wearing grass stained, white New Balance sneakers, white socks pulled halfway up his calves, khaki cargo shorts, and typically a hideously printed Hawaiian button-down shirt. Now, they weren't always Hawaiian prints, mind you. My personal favorite—that I myself gifted both Drew and Dad for Christmas several years ago—has brightly printed birds of paradise flowers on it, but superimposed between all those flowers are all of us kids' faces. And not just our smiling faces. Oh no. The aim of the game was to get a headshot with the wackiest and most obscene face we could manage. Marnie hates them, and Mom scolded all of us, but Dad and Drew loved them.

When Dad passed, Marnie had taken Dad's and had teddy bears made for Mom, Willow, Val, and myself out of the fabric. I hadn't seen Drew wear his since Dad's passing.

Today though—as usual for any kind of holiday or special gathering—I'm assuming Marnie had laid out clothes for Drew, because he has none of his usual tacky dad flair. Soft brown loafers that have seen better days adorn his feet, but his khaki slacks are clean and pressed, his red, white, and green plaid button down tucked neatly into his waistband.

"Merry Christmas kiddo," he says with a smile, reaching up and ruffling the hair on the top of my head. In his other hand he carries an oversized tote bag that's loaded down with wrapped gifts. Marnie carries a platter of cookies toward the kitchen, and then I can hear Mom's excited greeting. She's going to be a wreck today. Or blow the surprise with her excitement.

I glance down the hall at Willow, notching my chin toward Drew and then the door. She rolls her eyes, but snags Drew by twining her arm through his elbow and leading him toward the kitchen, too. "Merry Christmas, Uncle Drew!"

Once they're all out of view, I shove my feet into my snow

boots and bend over to lace them quickly. Snagging my coat off the rack by the door, I barely have my arms in when I'm swinging the door open to step outside.

I'm brought up short when I slam into a hard body, though. The air leaves my lungs in a whoosh and I stumble. One strong, muscular arm wraps around me and I feel more than hear the chuckle that rumbles out of the chest I'm pressed against.

The soft velvet against my cheek is decadent, and when my eyes focus, I realize I've just crashed into Santa.

Raising my eyes, I glare up into the twinkling blue eyes staring down at me, the corners crinkling with his wide, perfectly white smile.

"Ho Ho Ho, Noelle. Have you been a naughty girl this year?"

I open my mouth to snap at him, but my eyes snag on the arm he has raised above us. And then I see, pinched between his fingers, a sprig of mistletoe. The sharp retort dies on my lips as a delighted squeak escapes me.

I'm so happy I could kiss him.

So I do.

Chapter Nine

Theo

Noelle's hands clasp tightly on either side of my face, framing my jaw. Her fingers send jolts of electricity through every inch of my body—including straight to my dick—and I have to remember how to breathe. She yanks my face down toward her and I stop breathing altogether. Holy fuck.

Twisting my face in her hands, she turns my lips away from hers at the last second. Disappointment crashes through me and my stomach does this awful kamikaze dive that twists me all up. But at the first touch of her lips to my cheek, my heart thuds painfully in my chest. The arm still banded around her waist tightens reflexively, my hand spreading wide, spanning across her ribcage. Those lips—fuck that mouth that I've dreamed of kissing so many fucking times just like this, under these stupid mistletoes that my parents always insisted be strung up everywhere at Christmastime—brushes the corner of my mouth, and I'm fairly certain I black out for a heartbeat or two.

I could simply twist my head an inch and press my mouth to hers. She's so fucking close. Her scent wraps around me, sending my head into outer space. My dick is throbbing in my pants at having her so close... It takes every last ounce of my admittedly minimal self-control to not press my hips against hers. Fuck, I want her to feel me. Want her to know what she does to me. How she's always had this effect on me.

But then she's pulling away, clapping her hands excitedly, her wide, green eyes bright as she stares up at me. She reaches above us, waggling her fingers expectantly. "Oh my god, Theo, you are my hero! How'd you know I forgot the mistletoe?"

Fucking of course she forgot the mistletoe. I shake my head with a grin, but lower my arm to allow her to grasp it between her fingers. "There's never too much mistletoe at Christmas-time, Noe. I'll take any chance for Christmas kisses."

Stepping back, she lets her eyes drift over me from head to toe and I have to pray that she doesn't notice the erection that has to be tenting the front of the dark red velvet pants.

"You upgraded your Santa suit. Very nice," she says appreciatively, grinning as her eyes come back to mine. Flicking the white pompom attached to the tip of the matching Santa hat with her finger, she tilts her head, narrowing her eyes on me suspiciously. Glancing around me, she makes a show of looking for something. "What? No big Santa bag for you to stuff me into? Wasn't that your threat?"

Is she teasing me or flirting with me? Fuck, I can never tell with Noelle.

"It's still early, Santa wants to make sure you have time with the family before taking you away," I murmur, winking. She laughs, shaking her head, and then turns back into the house. As she shimmies her coat down her arms and toes her boots off, I ask, "Were you leaving?"

She turns to me, eyes wide, nose scrunched up, mouth twisted into a grimace. "I already told you—" she whispers, "—I forgot the mistletoe at the shop. I was headed out to go get it. But then you showed up; my knight in a velvet Santa suit."

I roll my eyes, following her as she tiptoes on red fuzzy socks toward the living room. But then she skips through to the study on the other side of the house, and I follow. She opens the glass paned French doors and walks in. The bookshelves are strung up with white Christmas lights, and a string has been attached to the center of the ceiling. Snagging the rolling office chair from behind her dad's desk, she wheels it to the center of the floor and then climbs up. The chair wobbles precariously, sliding several inches to the left and I lunge forward.

"Jesus, Noe," I mutter, clasping my hands around the arms of the chair to hold it steady as she straightens into a standing position. From my slightly crouched position, my face is level with the junction of her thighs. Glancing up her body, I watch as she reaches up to tie the mistletoe to the string suspended above her, stretching slightly as she does it. The pink sweater she's wearing —with bright red lettering reading 'FESTIVE AF' on the front—is loose fitting, and as she stretches, it comes away from her body, allowing my gaze to go straight up her shirt. I get a flashing glimpse of red lace at the undersides of her breasts—and something else at her waist that I don't get a good look at—and I'm pretty sure I black out again.

My cock is hard in my pants. I can't help it. She's too fucking beautiful. I lower my head, taking deep, steadying breaths. She wobbles from above me and on instinct I release my hold on the arms of the chair, wrapping both of my arms around the tops of her thighs as I straighten. She squeaks in alarm, her feet kicking out reflexively, and the wheeled office chair topples over onto its side on the hardwood floor.

Her hands find purchase on my shoulders, her fingers gripping tight into the velvet of the Santa coat. My cheek is pressed between her breasts now and I inhale deeply, her floral scent intoxicating to my senses. I can't help myself; I nuzzle my cheek against the softness of her chest, closing my eyes.

Fucking hell. Merry Christmas to me.

Chapter Ten

Noelle

O h my god.

Between the rush of panic from almost falling off the chair and the fact that Theo currently has his face smashed between my boobs, I'm finding it incredibly hard to breathe. Or to steady my pounding heart.

Or to convince Miss Kitty that this is *not appropriate*.

Because she's fucking loving this right now.

Bitch is practically purring.

"You okay?" Theo asks, his voice gruff and slightly muffled against my chest.

"Uh-huh," I mumble brokenly, my fingers tightening on his shoulders. I'm trying not to pant, attempting to force my breathing to steady. It's not working. "I'm fine." I swallow hard. "You?"

His arms squeeze around my thighs and it's then that I realize that one of his hands is fully cupping one of my ass cheeks, his thumb resting in the crease between them. My black leggings are thin and comfortable. *Did I mention that they're thin?* Heat blazes up my body, making my chest and face hot as the blush spreads. Theo's thumb is practically in the crack of my ass. Oh my god, I'm going to die of embarrassment. RIP to me.

"I'm good," he finally rasps. His thumb strokes the curve of my ass through the thin material of my leggings, just slightly. My eyelids flutter closed. *Oh holy night.*

"You can put me down now," I whisper, my voice coming out all trembly and breathy, but I can't help it. He nods against my chest, his nose rubbing against the inside curve of my boob and I can't stop the quiet gasp that escapes my throat at the sensation.

His arms loosen fractionally, allowing my body to slide down his. Slowly. Painfully, *erotically* slowly.

And then I feel it. Pressed up between my thighs as I slide down, lined up perfectly against me, and Miss Kitty is full on purring now. Because Theo is *hard*. So hard against me there's no mistaking it, or ignoring it.

Should I ignore it? What's the etiquette protocol for accidental boner rubbing? They don't teach this shit in the game of life handbook!

Should I pretend I don't feel that? This is just nature doing its nature-y thing when two bodies are pressed up against each other, right?

Right?!

He continues letting me slide down his body until my stockinged feet touch the floor again. Because of our height difference, that hardness is now cushioned against my stomach. I stare up at him, my eyes bouncing between his, then down to his mouth. His jaw is clenched shut tight; his lips pulled thin. But those eyes, those crystal blue eyes, are hot as they stare down at me.

"I'm so sorry," I whisper, my lips barely moving. I'm holding impossibly still, avoiding rubbing against him anymore than I already have. His throat bobs as he swallows hard. My heart trips over itself as his hands span across my hips, flexing, fingers digging into the softness above my butt.

"Just give me a second," he breaths, his voice low, gravelly. It hits me low in my belly, and Miss Kitty likes the way his voice skitters along every nerve ending, lighting me up like the lights strung up around the room. A rough, scoffing laugh escapes him, the corner of his mouth tilting up, and those eyes are back to twinkling mischievously. "One guess of what your present is."

73

Shoving away from him with my hands on his chest, I can't help the laugh that bubbles out of me. It breaks the tension from whatever the hell this is. I try—*I swear I fucking try*—to keep my eyes away from what's going on south of his beltline, but sweet baby Jesus...

Snapping my eyes back up to his, he winks, and my gaze is drawn down again as one of his hands flattens against the bulge between his legs. His eyebrows dip into a slight V and his teeth sink into the fleshy part of his bottom lip as an almost silent groan leaves his mouth. My mouth drops open, shamelessly watching that large hand press against the thickness beneath it.

"Angel, my eyes are up here," he whispers, and I blush fiercely at being caught. A grin tilts up his mouth, his blue eyes dancing. He tsks lightly, making me roll my eyes.

Dammit he's good looking. I noticed that before, right? My eyes flicker up to the mistletoe now hanging above us, then back to his mouth. His grin widens.

Stepping toward me, he tilts my face up with one finger beneath my chin. "Don't worry, I'll meet you under the mistletoe before the end of the night, Noelle."

And then he moves around me, disappearing out of the double French doors and into the hallway. Leaving me stunned and speechless... and ridiculously turned on.

Chapter Eleven

Theo

I make a detour into the bathroom as soon as I'm out of the study—because I cannot walk into the kitchen where both of our families are with a raging boner—and lean my hands on the bathroom sink. Hanging my head between my shoulders as I take in deep, steadying breaths, I focus on letting them out just as slowly.

Christ, I'm so hard it hurts. I'd been pressed right against her, right where I want to be the most, and the heat at the apex of her thighs had nearly done me in. I could have wrapped her legs around my waist. Could have ground up against her, letting her feel more, letting her feel just how fucking hard I am for her. Only for her. Always for her.

If those green eyes blown wide, that mouth falling open with those quick, panting breaths had been any indication, she liked what she'd felt. Her watching me palm my dick through my pants—through this stupid fucking Santa suit—had not helped in the slightest.

Palming myself again, I press down, willing my body to cooperate.

Part of me knows I should be embarrassed, or at the very least want to apologize, as I'd been raised to respect women... but I just can't. Because now Noelle knows. Or least is becoming aware of me as more than just her goofy fucking golden retriever bestie. And I refuse to let myself feel any embarrassment over how hard this woman makes me. I want her. I've wanted her for so long I can't remember a time I didn't.

I've wanted to kiss Noelle Compton under the mistletoe since we were twelve... and dammit, I'm going to. Tonight.

Chapter Twelve

Noelle

I can't keep my eyes off of Theo. All night. It's getting a little out of hand.

The man appeared in the kitchen after me, looking like we hadn't practically just dry humped in the study. Arms out wide, wearing that ridiculous Santa suit, the hat still on his head, he went around the room hugging everyone in greeting.

We ate dinner—Mom had gone all out on the feast, as usual—and then we migrated into the living room. Beau stoked the fire in the fireplace until it was roaring nicely, the crackle and snap of the logs drowned out by the laughter and chatter. Presents were handed out—by Theo, of course, he takes his Santa duties very seriously—and they were opened one by one.

I'm sitting on the floor, my back resting against the front of the couch where Willow is sitting behind me next to Luck. Mom is in the other corner of the couch, Beau and Val are snuggling in one of the oversized loveseats, and Drew and

Marnie have taken up seats in two cozy recliners. Glasses of wine and highballs of whisky are either half empty or just freshly refilled. I take a sip of my wine, watching my favorite people around the room.

Theo walks up in front of me, sinking down onto the floor directly next to me with a quiet groan as he folds his six-foot four body on the floor, leaning his back against the couch, too, forcing Luck to shift his knees to the side with a grumble about personal space. Our shoulders are nearly touching. He took the thick velvet Santa jacket and pants off a while ago, changing into a pair of well-worn jeans and that same long-sleeved t-shirt from this morning with the check boxes on it. The Santa hat is still on his head, though, slightly lopsided. His blonde hair peeks out from beneath the white fur trim, and my fingers ache to reach out and slide my fingers through his hair.

Fingers shaking with the sudden compulsion to touch him, I take another sip of my wine before glancing out of the corner of my eye at him. He grins down at me, holding out a red paper wrapped gift to me. It looks like a photo frame, like an eleven by fourteen inch. There's a white ribbon tied around it.

"You didn't have to get me anything," I murmur, setting my wine down on the floor next to me, then reach out and take the gift out of his hand. It's definitely a picture frame of some kind. I set it in my lap.

"Mmhmm. Just like you didn't have to get me anything, either," he grumbles, winking at me. "Those seats are going to be amazing."

I'd gotten us tickets to an NBA game, Detroit vs Chicago. He's over the moon.

"And those lightsaber chopsticks? Freaking amazeballs," he continued, bumping his shoulder into mine. "Perfect for our next Chinese night in."

"I got a pair, too," I laugh, leaning into his shoulder lightly. The heat of him sets my body ablaze and I try to steady my breathing at having him so close. When did all of this change? Do I want things to change between us?

"Jedi blue?" he asks, bringing me back. His gaze is narrowed down at me, eyes twinkling with mischief.

"Pfft. You know better than that. Dark Side all the way, baby."

"I don't know how we've managed to be friends all this time—"

I elbow him hard in the side and he grunts, but stops talking, as Beau pushes himself to his feet. Offering Val his hand, he says quietly, "Come with me for a second?"

Val sets her wine glass down on the end table next to her, uncurling her feet from beneath her legs. Beau helps her to her feet, and then the two of them disappear out of the living room and down the hallway.

We all wait a handful of seconds before every single one of us scrambles to our feet. We're trying to be quiet, but we're a giddy herd of half intoxicated elephants as we sneak down the hallway. Beau's left the double French doors leading into the study open, and we all crowd just in front the doorway against the wall, barely out of sight in the hall.

"Ooooh, is that mistletoe? Did you bring me in here just to kiss me, babe?" we hear Val murmur as we inch closer. I reach behind me and get an almost silent high five from Theo. He squeezes my fingers before letting them go. My fingers tingle clear up my arm.

I'm on my hands and knees on the floor, Theo is crouched half on top and half behind me, like in position to hike a football, one hand flat on the floor in front of me. I have to force my breathing to remain steady at having him so close against my back. Miss Kitty is back to purring, the horny bitch.

The white pompom on his hat swings forward, hitting me in the face and I swat at it and whisper-hiss, "Get your balls out of my face!"

I can feel his answering chuckle against my back where he's crouched, nearly touching me. *Is it hot in here? No? Just me? Okay, great.*

My mom shushes me from somewhere to my right as Beau starts talking. She sniffles, and I hear Willow next to her, handing her a tissue. We're stacked on top of one another like that episode of *FRIENDS* with all their heads stuck in Monica's apartment door. Out of the corner of my eye I see Marnie and Mom with their arms wrapped around each other in the darkness of the hall. They're both crying already, of course.

"Val, sweetheart, I've given a lot of thought to how I wanted to do this, how I wanted this night to go." We hear him take a deep breath in and exhale heavily. None of us can see them, hiding behind the frame of the door, but I can imagine it. And then Val's gasp reaches us, and I can't help it, my eyes tear up. Because I know Beau is down on one knee in front of my sister, and she's just realized what's happening. "You have been my girl for so long, Val, so much longer than I even knew. Taking you out for that Valentine's date was the best decision I've ever made... well, maybe second best, since this is probably my best decision—"

I'm inching forward, trying to peek around the doorframe when Theo wraps his free arm around my waist, hauling me back. His chest is flush against my back, and leans close to whisper low in my ear, "Hey, no cheating. Get back here."

"Calling you my girlfriend hasn't felt right, Val," Beau continues quietly, and my eyebrows dip into a V. "Please, sweetheart, let me have the honor of calling you my *wife*. I need the world to know that you are mine, and that I am yours. Forever. *Be mine*, sweetheart. Marry me."

"*I told him to say that—*" Theo whisper hisses in my ear. My elbow connects with his ribs and he groans quietly, tightening his arm around my middle in reflex.

"Shut up!" I hiss up at him. My words come out all shaky and breathy though, the contact of his hand spanning across my ribcage where his arm is circled around me making everything in my head fuzzy. His thumb is spanned wide on one side of my right breast, his fingers curling beneath the minimal curve, fingertips pressing into my ribs. His touch is lighting me up.

Mom shushes us both again and I hold my breath as Theo's fingers flex against my side, stroking lightly. He's got to be able to feel how hard my heart is pounding in my chest, his arm is pressed below where it's hammering away. I force myself to relax as we collectively hold our breaths, waiting. Until—

"Yes! Beau... *a million yesses*!" Val whispers, her voice

breaking. I swipe at the damn tears tracking down my cheeks. A rustle of movement and then the unmistakable sound of passionate kisses fill the air.

"Get your nosy asses in here, she said yes!" Beau calls out, his own deep voice rough with emotion. Mom and Marnie are rounding the door before the words are out of his mouth, followed by Drew, Willow, and Luck.

Theo's arm is still banded around my waist, that stupidly large hand still splayed wide, half spanning my ribs below my boobs and half across my side. His other hand is flat on the ground near my own hand as I'm still on my hands and knees. He presses his nose to the shell of my ear and I nearly faint. *Holy. Shit.* His breath mists my ear as he whispers low, "Are you crying, Noelle?"

"Pfft," I mutter, my voice shaking. Then, I grumble admittedly, "*Yes.*"

"Good, me too," he whispers, then pushes himself to his feet, hauling me up with him. My ass connects with his lap as we straighten and he grunts, pressing his hand to my stomach to steady me. "Christ, you're going to be the death of me, woman."

Same, buddy. Fucking same.

Chapter Thirteen

Theo

Keeping myself from dragging Noelle down the hallway, away from the rest of our families, takes all of my willpower. Straightening from crouching over her, with her ass damn near pressed against my lap, just to have that ass land fully against me as we stood up... I'm toast. Done. Stick a fucking fork in me. I don't want to play anymore tonight.

I want her, alone, her mouth underneath mine, my hands on every inch of her body.

I do none of those things, though. I take a deep, steadying breath in and follow her into the study where the rest of our families are crowding around Beau and Val. Mom and Aunt Rachel are dabbing at their eyes, fawning over the glittering diamond now perched on Val's left hand and giving Beau celebratory hugs. My dad claps Beau on the back, beaming over at him. Willow and Noelle are hugging Val as she holds her hand out to show off the ring Beau picked out.

I step over to my brother and clap him on the back, too.

"Congrats, man. Happy for you."

"Thanks, Theo," Beau says, his dark eyes crinkling at the corners. "You'll be my best man, right?"

My eyebrows shift up in surprise. "Uhh, yeah. I'd be honored, man."

I'm not going to lie; I'm shocked as hell. I mean, don't get me wrong, my brother and I are close, but I've always just assumed he thought I was his annoying dumbass younger brother.

He nods his head, lips pulling into a smile, then turns back to his new fiancé. Noelle skips over to me, fairly bouncing. "Okay, totally worth all the trouble and almost dying."

I chuckle, draping one arm around her shoulders and pulling her into my side. The move is natural, something I've never thought twice about before. Now, my fingers tingle as I trail them over her bicep, over the softness of her sweater. Her other arm slides around my waist, her fingers spanning in the space between my ribcage and hipbone. Physical contact has never been awkward for us... but Christ I'm struggling now. Having my hand on her ass her earlier, standing almost exactly where we are now, my face buried in her tits, with my cock pressed up against the cleft of her thighs... All of those things are making this so much fucking harder now.

Among other things.

Releasing my hold on her shoulder, I drift my hand down and twine my fingers through hers. She glances up at me, her lips parting just slightly. The only light in the study is that of the Christmas lights strung up around the room, and it makes her eyes shine like stars.

I'm barely aware of our families leaving the room, heading back to the living room or kitchen. All I can do is stare down at her, my heart a jackhammer in my chest. Backing up several steps, I pull her with me, until we're back beneath the mistletoe again.

It's now or never.

Chapter Fourteen

Noelle

"What are you doing?" I whisper, my breath coming out in quick, shallow pants. The look in his eyes... it's intense, heated. Gone is the lighthearted, goofy guy Theo, and in his place... I swallow hard. "Theo..."

His blue eyes search mine for what feels like an eternity as we stand together, his fingers clasped tightly around mine. His gaze is so intense and alive with a fire that smolders in the blue depths, the twinkle of the Christmas lights that are strung throughout the room reflected in his eyes. That ridiculous Santa hat still on his head, and it looks unfairly sexy on him. His voice is low, gruff as he whispers, "I told you I'd meet you under the mistletoe."

"Theo, I thought that was a joke, making fun of that post Willow made—"

"I may joke about a lot of things, be the loveable goofball that no one takes seriously... but I would never joke about kissing you, Angel."

Eyes blazing, he stares down at me, and I can feel the heat radiating off of him as he presses closer. His hand leaves mine, traveling up my arm and up, up until his hand is bracketing the front of my throat. His touch is gentle but sure, his strong fingers tilting my chin up. I glance up at the mistletoe hanging above us.

My heart is fairly galloping in my chest at his huskily spoken words and I lick my lips. Bringing my gaze back to his, he breathes, "Not when I've wanted to for as long as I can remember…"

He ducks his head just slightly, his lips brushing along my jaw and electricity zings through every nerve in my body at the contact. My mouth falls open with a gasp, and his lips move across my cheek. I'm panting, my entire body trembling. His lips hover over the corner of my mouth and I shift slightly, tilting my head just a touch, as much as his hand bracketing my jaw will allow. His breath grazes my mouth, his lips fluttering lightly over mine.

"…Theo," I breathe, my lips parting. Oh holy night, I want this. So bad.

"I'm going to kiss you, Noelle. I've thought about kissing you under these damn mistletoes every single Christmas Eve since we were twelve. So, I'm going to kiss you, right here, right now. Like I've always wanted to," he rasps, his voice thick and growly, his lips moving against mine. Not quite touching but enough to make my body feel like it's on fire. He smells like cinnamon and pine, the scent dancing around me, enveloping me until it's all I can smell, his breath fanning across my cheeks and lips again. That hand at my throat tightens just marginally and I sigh out a breathy moan. His other hand is at my hip now, fingers digging into the softness there. "So, if you don't want me to kiss you, now would be the optimal time to knee me in the balls. Because once I start, I'm not stopping, Noe."

His blue eyes are heavy lidded as he stares down at me, waiting. Giving me the chance to say no.

Sliding my hands up his sides, I spread my fingers wide against his ribs beneath his arms. "Kiss me, Theo—"

His fingers tightening at my throat, he groans, crushing his mouth to mine. He wastes no time, parting his lips and sliding his tongue out to find my lips already open and waiting for him.

At the first touch of his tongue to mine, I gasp, arching my body against his. His hand at my waist slides around to sit low on my back, just above the curve of my ass, but then his hand is sliding down to cup me fully, hauling me close against him. I feel him, hard and heavy and full, against my belly.

He kisses me like a man given his last meal, his lips and tongue fierce and greedy but generous. Fucking hell, the man knows how to kiss. He nips my lower lip with his teeth and raging desire flashes through me. Miss Kitty is ecstatic.

Rocking against his front, I moan around his kiss, heat scorching me. I'm wet and aching.

"Christ, Noelle," he breathes, releasing my mouth and pressing his forehead to mine. "I don't want to stop."

"Don't stop," I plead, tilting my head and pressing my mouth to his again. "Don't you dare stop."

He chuckles, the sound low and dark and it skitters over me, making me shiver. "Yeah?"

I nod frantically, as much as that hand at my neck will let me. "Come over tonight."

His fingers tighten, squeezing this time, forcing my chin up so he can stare at me. He's squeezing just tight enough to restrict my airway, but not enough to close it completely. It's thrilling and so fucking sexy my knees threaten to buckle. Who is this man? I'm loving this side of Theo.

"You better think real hard on that, Angel," he rasps, his words gravelly. "Because if I come over tonight... You understand what's going to happen, right?"

I swallow, the motion stilted slightly with his hand collaring my throat the way it is. I nod. He bites down on his lower lip, a growl rumbling up his throat. I tremble.

"I'm going to fuck you, Noelle. I'm going to fuck you exactly how I've wanted to, and you're going to take it, aren't you?"

"Holy shit," I moan on a stilted breath. His fingers loosen and I suck in a full breath, my head buzzing. *Oh, that's hot. Yes please.*

"Say it, Noelle," he rasps, tilting my face up to his again.

"Yes, Theo."

"Yes, what?" he asks, trailing his lips along mine. I shudder with arousal and anticipation.

"I want you to fuck me."

His approving growl lights me up from the inside out, like those damn lights twinkling everywhere. *I. Am. Unwell.*

"Are you wet for me, Angel?" he asks. The hand at my back moves, sliding around until he's cupping me through my leggings. His fingers find my clit through the thin material and I gasp, rocking into his hand. I nod frantically. "Fucking Christ, I can feel how hot and wet you are through these. I can't wait to feel it, taste it. You're going to come so hard for me you're not going to remember your own name, baby."

Normally, if a man talked like that to me, I'd haul off and

punch him. It's cocky and arrogant...and I have no fucking doubt that he means every word. Damn this Theo is hot as hell.

"Go get your things and say your goodnights," he says before kissing me again. Thorough and hungry.

He releases me completely, stepping back. I stumble at the loss of contact, my knees shaking. He raises his hand, drawing his thumb over my lips, and my breath catches in my throat as his next words reach my ears.

"I've wanted to do this for so fucking long, Noelle. I've wanted you forever."

Chapter Fifteen

Noelle

I'm *Theo's mystery girl.*

The realization crashes through me as I stumble my way out of the study and down the hallway. My lips feel kiss swollen and I drag my fingers over them, as if by touching them I can go back and live that all over again. Because good lord, the man can kiss.

I'm Theo's mystery girl. The one he said didn't know he existed... the one he said the timing wasn't right with...

Wait, I am his mystery girl, right? I suppose he could have been talking about someone else last night. He could just be saying all of this as a trick to get some easy ass.

Shaking my head even as the ridiculous thought starts, I know that isn't it. Theo isn't a playboy, a use-em-and-lose-em kinda guy. He isn't just going to say pretty words to get a woman into bed, especially me. Our relationship—hell, our friendship—is currently balancing precariously on the precipice of a life-altering change. He wouldn't be saying this, doing this, if he didn't mean it. Our friendship runs too deep, has for too long, to chance ruining it just for some easy sex.

No, I believe every word that came out of his mouth. And it's opened my eyes to what has been there this whole time. He's wanted me for a long time.

I'm happy to oblige. If he's as talented at the rest of it as he is at kissing... I just may cease to be part of this earth tonight. But what a helluva way to go.

I'm still half dazed when I make my way back to the kitchen where our families are congregated around the kitchen counter. I picked up my wine on my way through the living room and take a sip of it as I look around the kitchen. Mom and Marnie are hugging each other again. I know they're both overjoyed with tonight. They've both waited a long time for this, even though this is Val's second marriage... no one liked that cheating asshole ex-husband of hers anyway.

What's that saying about marriages? Oh yeah, they're like pancakes. You can always throw the first one out.

I scoff to myself at my own little joke and cough to cover it as they all turn to look at me. "Sorry," I wheeze, thumping my chest, holding up my wine glass for show. "Swallowed wrong."

I sense Theo come up behind me then. As our families

turn back to what they were doing, he leans in close, his lips brushing the shell of my ear. His breath is warm, rustling the hair at my temple as he whispers, "You'll swallow everything I give you tonight, Angel."

"*Theo*—" I hiss on a whisper between my clenched teeth, my face flaming at his bold, dangerous words. Butterflies erupt in my belly though. Because good lord, I want that. Yes please.

He chuckles, quiet and low and it sends shivers along my spine. His hands span my waist, settling between my ribs and my hip bones, and he squeezes once before stepping around me.

"I'm going to head home," he announces to the room. Everyone turns toward him, and they all in turn give him good-bye hugs and final 'Merry Christmas' wishes. He turns toward me then, his blue eyes twinkling mischievously. "The snow is still coming down pretty hard. Want me to give you a ride home? You've had several glasses of wine."

"Oh, what a good idea," Marnie says, nodding along with Mom.

"Thank you, Theo," Mom said, patting his arm with a smile. "You've always been such a good boy."

I roll my lips in between my teeth to keep from laughing out loud. I choke on the laugh though, coughing for real this time when his eyes find mine. The mischievous twinkle is gone from his eyes and that heated, burning gaze is back in full force.

"Come on, you lush, let's get you home before you turn into a pumpkin." His tone is teasing, but that look in his eyes is anything but. It makes me shiver again.

I cock one hip out and tilt my head up to look at him, my brows raised. "I'm no Cinderella."

He steps closer, our family blissfully ignorant to the heat and tension radiating between the two of us. "Is there a princess that gets tied up and spanked for her smart mouth?"

"I'm not sure Disney would sanction that—"

He grips the point of my chin between his thumb and pointer finger, pushing my head up further. I can feel my pulse fluttering wildly in my neck, my chest. My breaths are choppy, though I'm trying my damndest to keep it steady. "I have a better way to handle this smart mouth, Noelle. By stuffing my cock between these lips and fucking your throat."

My eyes widen and my mouth drops open in surprise. I lick my lips, my heart beating like a fucking drum in my ears. I'm both nervous and outrageously turned on at his filthy threat. Instinctively, I clench my thighs together to relieve some of the ache he's built there.

And, being the smart-ass that I am, I whisper, "Prove it."

Chapter Sixteen

Theo

The smile that pulls at my lips at her taunting whisper is wolfish at best. The woman has no idea what's waiting for her when we get to her place. And she's just given me the go-ahead.

Noelle Compton is mine tonight.

Fucking finally.

"Good night, family," I call over my shoulder, pushing Noelle away from me before anyone sees just how close we are, the way our bodies are angled in toward each other, the way her hands tremble just slightly as she sets her wine glass down on the counter next to us.

"Do you need help carrying anything out?" Beau asks, stepping toward us.

I glance over my shoulder, giving him my best goofy grin and shake my head. "Nah. I got it. Thanks though."

Noelle is back in the living room, gathering the gifts she'd received, my gift to her still wrapped where she'd left it when we'd all scrambled to follow Beau and Val earlier. Christ, it feels like a lifetime ago now.

"Do you want me to open this now?" she asks, holding up the flat gift. I shake my head, bending to pick up the gifts I'd been given as well. I snag one of the larger gift bags tossed into the corner of the room and start loading both our things into it. We'll separate them later. Right now, I need to get her home and naked.

"You can open it later." I pluck it out of her hands, sliding it into the gift bag. Clasping the front of her throat in my hand loosely, I tilt her face up toward mine. Seeing the way her pupils blow wide and that perfect pink mouth dropping open at the little show of dominance has my cock thickening behind the fly of my pants. Christ, I've been half hard most of the night. "I have something to prove first, don't I, Angel?"

She simply nods, staring up at me. This is going to be fun. Corrupting my little Christmas Angel.

"Let's go, Noelle."

We're out in the hallway, slipping on jackets and boots, and then I grab her hand and pull her out the door with me. The snow hasn't slowed in the slightest, and my car is already half buried in the white fluff. I make sure she gets into the passenger seat, hand her my keys, and then place the bag of our gifts in the back, grabbing the snow brush off the backseat at the same time. As I clear off the back window, I see her lean over the console and start the ignition, then adjust the thermostat. I make my way around the vehicle, brushing the snow off as quick as I can, then slide into the driver's seat. Tossing the snow brush behind us, I look over at her as she turns to face me, her eyes hooded and those pink lips parted just slightly.

"Fuck it," I mutter, grabbing hold of her face and pulling her across the console toward me.

The inside of the car is still cold and her skin is cool against my fingers, but the air is blowing full blast, and I know within minutes it's going to be nice and toasty in here. Her mouth crashes into mine, and I don't hesitate a second to push my tongue between her lips. The throaty, muffled moan that escapes her is music to my ears. We kiss until we're both breathless, and then I kiss her some more. I can't stop. I've wanted this, wanted her, for so fucking long. I already know that tonight is going to fucking ruin me.

"Holy shit," she whispers when I finally pull away, dragging the pad of my thumb across her now kiss swollen bottom lip. I press my forehead against hers, rolling it there several times as I work to reign in my need for her. "Theo."

"*Fuck* I love the way you say my name like this," I rasp,

dragging my mouth across hers again. "I've waited a lifetime to hear my name on your lips this way. So desperate and needy and all fucking *mine*, Noelle."

She nods against my mouth, and I chuckle darkly through the interior of the car. My little angel has no idea what's coming when we get to her place.

Chapter Seventeen

Noelle

He drives with one hand slung over the steering wheel, the other clasped firmly around my thigh just above my knee. The heat of his palm through the thin leggings is like a branding iron to my skin. I'm starting to realize that things will never be the same between Theo and me... he's going to ruin me, I just know it.

Theo drives cautiously through the quiet, night darkened streets, the snow still coming down like crazy. When he pulls us into the driveway at my house, there's no tire marks. Belle is gone for the holiday, spending it with her family a couple towns over. The house is dark and quiet, just the colorful Christmas lights strung up in the windows. I'm trying—and failing miserably—to control my breathing and the rapid thu-dunk of my heart in my chest. Theo puts his car in park and shuts off the engine, and then he's reaching for me again.

His warm palm on the back of my neck scorches me down

to my toes as he drags me across the console again, kissing me. God, kissing Theo is like nothing I've ever experienced. He's thorough and demanding and holy holly berries, it's just *so good*.

I try not to let myself think about how he got so good at this. All the other women that have enjoyed this side of Theo... He was standing just in front of me this entire time, and I was too blind to see it.

"When we get inside, I want these clothes off, understood?" he rasps against my mouth, his voice dark and demanding. I shiver, despite the heat still radiating through the interior of the car. "Everything but your panties and bra."

I nod, my lips dragging against his, and then he's gone, sliding out of the driver's side door. I push open the passenger door, stepping out into the ankle-deep snow as he rounds the hood of the car. He extends his hand to me and I slip my hand into his, his long, tapered fingers twining closed around mine as he drags me to the front door. I'm laughing as we push inside the house, but the laughter dies abruptly.

His hands bracket my face and tip it upward to allow his mouth to cover mine, cutting off the laughter and every halfway coherent thought except for '*Yes*'. His body is pressed fully against mine, my back flat against the closed door. We're ravenous for each other. My need for him is unparalleled, and my fingers fist into the hem of his shirt, yanking on it.

"You first," he pants, breaking his mouth from mine. "I want to see you. Fuck, Noelle. I need to see you."

His hands drop to my jacket, shoving it off my shoulders and down my arms. I'm kicking off my boots as gracefully as I can with his body still anchoring me to the door. My boots are kicked away at the same time my jacket falls to the floor, and then his hands are at my leggings, yanking them down my thighs. He kneels on one knee, pulling the leggings off my feet. He sucks in a breath as his palms slide up the outside of my thighs as he stands. Theo's hands catch the hem of my sweatshirt as he rises, pulling it up and over my head in one fluid motion.

I shake my long, wavy hair as it falls back around my shoulders, and he takes a step back from me. His blue eyes are blazing hot as they trail over every inch of me. My sweatshirt falls from his fingers to the floor in a heap.

"Jesus help me," he breathes, his gaze scorching as it travels over my body before raising back to mine. I shiver, anticipation settling low in my belly. "Have you had this on all night?"

Nodding, I blush, the heat making my cheeks flame.

He reaches out one hand, his fingers trailing over the red

lace edge of my bralette before they slide down between my breasts, to the garter belt that's strapped around my waist, then lower to the lacy edge of the matching thong. It's totally impractical and I honestly have no other excuse for wearing the matched set other than pure vanity and wanting to feel pretty. But damn am I glad I did, because the look on Theo's face right now is totally worth it.

"Who did you wear this for, Noelle?" he asks, his voice dropping low.

I shrug one shoulder, the blush creeping down my chest as embarrassment nearly chokes me. "No one."

His jaw clenches. "You just decided to put this on for the hell of it? Who were you going to see later tonight?"

I'm taken aback by the harshness of his tone, but then I smile when the realization hits me. "Are you jealous, Theo?"

"Damn right I'm jealous," he breathes, his fingers digging into the band of the garter belt. "Fuck, no one else gets to see you like this, Angel. This is for me."

I raise one brow at him. "You think you can go all caveman on me, Theo?"

He leans forward, his mouth grazing over the corner of my upturned lips. "You haven't seen caveman behavior yet. But keep that smart mouth up, and I'll show you how I handle brats."

"You're a lot of talk, but I haven't seen anything to back your game," I breathe, taunting him. His dark, deep chuckle sends shivers down my spine, and I know I've just awoken the bear. Finally.

"If you move, I will bend you over and mark this ass up until it's the same red as these—" he whispers, fingering the garter belt at my waist. "And if you don't believe me, try me."

He backs away, leaving me against the door, and I stay where I am, trembling.

"Good girl," he praises, his voice low and thick. I damn near melt. He strips his clothes off, his shirt piling to the floor next to mine, and then he's working at the buttons and zipper of his jeans at the same time that he toes off his boots.

His cock is hard and thick, straining against a pair of black, tight boxer briefs. My mouth drops open slightly at the sight. I can't wait to see all of him. Wrap my fingers around the length of him, take him in my mouth—

"Don't move," he warns huskily as he kicks his jeans away. "Or do. I'd love to punish you for being naughty, Angel."

I remain where I am, still trembling. My chest is rising and falling rapidly as I watch him walk over to the nearest window. Leaving the lights plugged in, he starts removing the strand from where it's taped to the perimeter of the window, winding the strand to keep it from tangling. I'm transfixed, watching as the muscles in his forearm bunch with the movements.

"Come here."

"Is this a trick to get me to move and then you get to spank me?" I tease, pressing my back more firmly against the door.

"That mouth of yours is going to do that for you," he responds, finally turning his head toward me. I bite my lower lip to keep from smirking. He raises his eyebrows at me, then growls, "Now, Noelle."

Feeling feisty, I give him a mock salute and quip, "Yes, sir."

I push away from the door, moving slowly toward him. He directs me to stand in front of him so that I'm facing the window. It's frosted at the edges from the cold outside. The snow is coming down harder than before, the heavy, fat flakes making it almost impossible to see to the street beyond.

Theo presses his chest into my back, one hand snaking up to wrap around my throat from behind. His fingers are firm, but not tight enough to hurt or to fully restrict my oxygen. It's primal and sexy and so unlike the Theo that I've known all my life. It's thrilling. The trembling intensifies as his other hand manacles one of my wrists, pulling it behind my back, before reaching for the other one.

His fingers tighten slightly around my throat and then his lips move along my hairline as his breath ghosts over the shell of my ear. "I may be the goofy guy that no one takes seriously out there, Noelle, but when we're in here, I need you to understand that I know what I want and I will have what I want. And right now, I'm dying to tie you up and fuck you seven ways to Sunday." His teeth nip at a spot along my neck below my ear and I can't stop the gasping, throaty moan that leaves me. Holy shit. My lower body clenches with anticipation. "I can't wait to feel you come, to hear it, to watch it."

"Oh my god, Theo." I'm practically panting from arousal. My teeth sink into my bottom lip as I tilt my head back against his shoulder. He presses his hardness against my ass and I can't stop myself from grinding my hips against him. Theo Collins is a filthy talker and it's making me fucking *melt*.

The hand that is manacling both of my wrists behind my back shifts at the same time that he releases my throat. The heat of him at my back disappears as he steps back slightly, and then my mouth drops open when I feel it; he winds the strand of still lit Christmas lights around my wrists. He continues, twining the strand around my arms, then across my body, down my thighs, until I'm tied up completely. I glance down my body as he works, the colorful bulbs lighting against my skin. Raising my eyes, I follow his movements in the reflection of the dark window, the lights showing up starkly in the dark.

"Guess you were right about Santa kidnapping me tonight, huh?" I ask on a nervous giggle, my eyes tracking him in the reflection in the window. I wiggle my wrists, testing the rigidity of the lights bound around them. He's got me tied up good and tight, though I realize he must know what he's doing because they're not too tight. Jealousy streaks through me and my mouth opens before I can stop it, the words biting as they fall out of me. "Do I want to know how you got so good at this?"

"Boy scouts," is all he says from behind me, but his hand is back at my throat now, collaring it and turning my face toward his. I'm not entirely sure I believe him. He smirks. "Who's jealous now, Angel?"

I reach for his mouth with mine, then whine when he pulls back before I can kiss him. "*Theo.*"

"I told you that smart mouth of yours was going to get you into trouble," he murmurs, trailing his mouth down the side of my neck, before sinking his teeth into the meaty part of my shoulder. I cry out at the sharp pain, but then his tongue is soothing it and I can't stop from shaking against the bonds that are holding me captive. "You've been naughty all night,

Noelle. Get on your knees. I'm going to show you what happens to brats."

His hand is still firmly clasped around my throat as I lower to my knees, and then he's moving around me, standing in front of me. With my hands firmly tied behind my back, I can't touch any of him, and I hate it. He tips my face up with a finger beneath my chin as he ducks, pressing his mouth to mine, before he straightens.

"Pull your cock out, I want to see it," I breathe, my gaze fixed on the hard bulge behind his underwear. He chuckles from above me and I raise my eyes to his, glaring. "What?"

"It's just funny, that you think you're going to call the shots," he whispers, his blue eyes taunting. "You don't get to top from the bottom, Angel."

Oh. Fuck.

"For that, you don't get to see what's about to happen," he murmurs, stepping back away from me. He pushes on my shoulders until I'm no longer on my knees, but resting with my butt on the backs of my heels. My heart picks up it's pounding in my chest. "The more you brat, Noelle, the harder this is going to be for you."

I watch as he walks away, back toward the door. He plucks a scarf from the row of hooks by the door, sliding the soft material through his fingers as he returns, standing behind me again. He tips my head back, leaning over me to kiss me fiercely again, leaving me breathless. Then he's sliding the scarf over my eyes, securing it behind my head so that I'm completely blindfolded, and the only thing I can do is listen, now. It's terrifying and thrilling, handing him this power over me.

My ears strain, listening for him. The rustle of fabric, and then the sound of skin on skin, a low groan. My mouth parts, and my imagination goes haywire. Is he stroking his cock? Fuck, I wish I could see.

"Here's what's going to happen, Angel," he whispers, his voice so low and guttural it sends shivers down my body. My nipples are hard, straining against the lace of my bralette. I hear a jingle, then startle when something cold and metal is placed in my palm. A jingle bell off the mini tree. "You're going to hold onto that tight. I'm going to fuck this smart mouth, and you're going to take all of it, aren't you?" I nod, moaning at his filthy words. My thong is soaked, I'm so wet and aching. "You were naughty, Noelle. So now you're tied up and blindfolded, and with my cock between these lips—" his fingers trail over my mouth and I open instinctively, "—you won't be able to talk. That bell in your hand is your call. If you need a breath, or for me to stop, you ring that bell, understood?"

I nod again, and he chuckles from above me.

"Such a greedy girl," he rasps, and I sigh out another moan. Good god, the mouth on this man. "Open for me."

I drop my jaw and stick out my tongue, which earns me a growling, guttural groan from Theo in appreciation.

"Such a pretty sight," he whispers, and then the tip of his cock is at my waiting tongue. "Lick it, Noelle. Put that smart mouth to good use."

Normally, I would bristle at the derogatory command, but coming from Theo, in that desperate rasp, I'm lost, and all I want to do is exactly what he's telling me to do. Wrapping my lips around him, I moan as he sinks in. His hands bracket my head, holding me still as he moves, slow, shallow thrusts. I swirl my tongue around the head of him, earning another low groan. I clutch the bell in my hand, curling my fingers around it tightly so it doesn't make a sound. Hallowing my cheeks, I suck him in and moan around him as the tip touches the back of my throat. I relax my throat, allowing him deeper as he picks up pace, his fingers tightening in my hair.

"Oh, fuck," he groans low. His fingers sweep along my cheek then down to my chin, tenderly, almost reverently. It's a direct contradiction to the dominant nature that seems to be coming out to play. His fingers glide along my bottom lip.

"Goddamn, you look so good like this. I love watching these lips take my cock. Can you take all of it?" I try to nod, humming around him. He pushes deeper, making me gag before he pulls back slightly, allowing me to breathe. "Good girl, good girl. Take a breath. Try again?"

I nod, and when he pushes deep this time, I'm ready for him, relaxing my throat. His guttural, fierce growl from above me makes me practically feral. God I wish I could see him. I want to touch him. I'm so wet I'm aching, and I clench my thighs together to try and relieve the painful ache there. I want him to touch me. I need to come.

"Jesus Christ, Noelle," he pants, pulling back so that he can thrust shallowly again. "You needy thing. Look at you, you're so wet, aren't you? You love taking this cock down your throat?" I nod again. He grunts, thrusting long and slow. "I want to keep fucking your mouth but I don't want to come yet. I want to come with my cock in that greedy pussy."

I feel his fingers at the back of my head, and then the blindfold is falling away. I blink my eyes into focus, raising my eyes up his incredible body until they collide with the intense blue of his own.

"Goddamn," he groans, throwing his head back to stare at the ceiling before dropping his chin and piercing me with his stare again. "You're fucking perfect."

Chapter Eighteen

Theo

Those are not the three words I want to say to her right now.

But I know that telling a woman that I love her while my cock is buried in her mouth isn't the most romantic way to say it for the first time. So I grit my teeth and let my eyes say it for me, knowing she won't know what I'm trying to say. Not entirely, anyway. Though I think she's starting to understand.

"Is that pussy wet for me?" I ask, my chest heaving. God, I want to come so bad, spill down her throat, watch her take all of it and then kiss the shit out of her and taste myself there. Noelle stares up at me with those heavy lidded, lust-filled jade eyes, and nods, humming around the length of me still buried between her lips. She looks so fucking pretty all tied up and bound, just taking everything that I'm giving to her. She's going to look so good coming for me. "Do you want me to fuck you with my tongue, Angel?"

She hums again, nodding. I groan, the vibrations at the

back of her throat almost sending me over the edge. Fuck, this is heaven. This moment with this woman. I never thought we'd be here. Not really. Goddamn, I'm glad we are though.

I pop my dick out of her mouth, then trail the swollen head over her lips while she pants for breath. "You did so good, Noe. Are you ready to come on my tongue?"

"Jesus, Theo," she breathes, staring up at me with those wide eyes, before dropping her gaze to my cock, still gripped in one hand while I pump it slowly. Her mouth drops open again, then her teeth bite down on her lower lip. Fuck. I want to give her everything. Forever. This woman has the ability to wreck me completely, and I have no interest in stopping it from happening. "I want to come on your cock."

I chuckle at that. "Oh, you will be," I rasp. "Multiple times, Noelle. I told you, you won't remember your own name by the time I'm done with you."

"You're so unbelievably cocky," she scoffs, raising her eyes back to mine tauntingly. My brows lower and I narrow my eyes at her. Fucking brat just doesn't know when to stop. Just another one of the things that I love about her. She keeps me on my toes.

"You really like being tied up, don't you?" I ask, leaning down to collar her throat with my hand again, notching her chin up and toward me. I lean in until our mouths are barely brushing against each other, so that when I speak my lips move against hers. "Keep bratting, Noelle. I can do this all fucking night."

She moans, the sound vibrating against my palm where it's pressed against her throat. Fuck I like that.

Placing my hands beneath her armpits, I lift her to her feet. She groans, stretching her knees out. I grin, tilting her face up to mine again. "It's really too bad this cord isn't longer. I really would like to keep you tied up while I make you come with my tongue."

But I unwind the string of lights from around her body, her legs, her arms. I kiss my way along each indent that the plastic cord made across her skin, then drop the lights in a heap by the wall. Her hands are on me the instant she's free, fingers sliding up through my hair as I stand, taking her mouth with mine once more. I lift her easily, wrapping her arms and legs around me as I stride toward the bedroom. I can't wait any longer to have her.

I drop her onto the bed, still rumpled from where she'd probably scrambled out of it this morning, late for work. She laughs as she lands, bouncing slightly, but the laugh dies when I lower myself to my knees by the side of the bed, dragging her toward the edge. Spanning my hands wide across the inside of her thighs, I lean in, trailing my nose and lips across the red scrap of lace that's covering what I can't wait to discover. Her hands are in my hair, holding me tight.

"Theo," she whimpers, and I can't get enough of the way my name sounds on her lips like this.

I grip the band of her panties in both hands and pull them down. She raises her hips enough to allow me to get them out from beneath her ass, and then I'm dragging the scrap of material down her thighs, tossing them aside. I leave the garter belt at her waist and the bra covering her tits, for now, at least. I'll get to those later.

Right now, fuck. This pretty pink pussy is waiting for me. "So pretty and soaked for me, Angel," I rasp, sliding my fingers along the wetness that glistens between those folds. Leaning forward, I lap my tongue against the bud of her clit and she jerks as a gasp erupts out of her.

Wrapping my arms around her thighs, I spread her wide and drape her legs over my shoulders, then I feast. Fuck, she's delicious.

Long strokes of my tongue into her pussy, quick flicks against her clit that have her thighs spasming against my shoulders. I close my lips around her clit and suck as I flick it with my tongue and she trembles wildly, her hands frantic in my hair. Her cries are pure music to my ears, that husky, needy moan mixed with the higher pitched ones that have my cock leaking at the tip.

"Theo, Theo—" she calls, her hands flattening against the sides of my head. I'm watching her from between her thighs, my gaze pinned to her face as she tosses her dark head back and forth against the bed. I hum against her clit. She's close, I can feel it. "Yes, right there, right there—"

Her stomach muscles contract and her back bows off the bed entirely, and then she's coming. I drink her in, savoring every pulse of her clit and pussy against my tongue, every gasping cry that escapes her lips. And it's my name that she calls as she comes. My name. Like it should have always been.

Releasing one thigh, I drop my arm so that I can slide two fingers deep inside. She's still pulsing, little aftershocks, and I flick my fingers against that little spot inside. I lift my head as she sobs. "That's it, Noe. Keep coming, baby. Soak my face."

And then I return to her, clamping my lips and teeth around her clit again. Her entire body goes stiff as she comes again, harder this time, and I grunt against her clit, my teeth still nipping lightly as she spasms around my fingers that are pressed deep. "Theo, Theo, Theo!"

Once I'm satisfied that she's sated, at least for a moment, I rise, shoving my boxers the rest of the way down my legs until I can kick them away.

"How attached are you to this garter and bra?" I growl. She pants, her head thrashing against the bed as she continues to come down from her high.

"Huh?" she asks, her mouth open with each panting breath she sucks in.

"I need them off, now. How attached are you to this set?" I ask again, reaching for the scrap of lace at her waist.

"I mean I like them—"

"I'll buy you new ones." My fingers tear the lace off of her, then do the same to the flimsy lace that is still covering her tits. It splays open and she gasps in shock.

"I can't believe you just did that," she laughs, glancing down at her now naked body. She's fucking stunning. Every smooth, lithe, pale inch of her. Bracing myself over her with my hands on either side of her, I drop my mouth to one nipple. Her tits are small, always have been, but goddamn, these nipples have been part of my spank bank material for years. She arches off the bed, her fingers tunneling through my hair and holding tight, before I switch to the other one.

"Theo, please," she whispers from above me. "Please. Fuck

me."

I shake my head, dragging my lips over her nipple. "Yeah, that's not what's going to happen, Noelle."

She grips my hair tighter, tugging my mouth away from her body. "What the fuck?"

Crawling over her, I settle myself between her parted thighs, then lower my body until I'm leaning against one forearm. I cup her cheek with my other hand and lean in to kiss her gently. My heart is hammering in my chest at what I'm about to say. But I can't not say it.

"I can't just fuck you, Noelle. I need you to understand that's not all this is for me," I breathe, staring at her with every ounce of emotion that's roiling through me.

"Oh," she whispers slowly, her mouth parting in an 'O'. She stares up at me, her green eyes shimmering. She traces her fingers along my temple, my cheek, my lips. She nods slowly, a small smile pulling at her lips. "*Theo...*"

I clasp her hand in mine and bring her fingers to my lips, kissing them. We continue to stare at each other over our clasped fingers. "Always, Angel. It's always been you."

Noelle pulls our hands toward her own mouth, kissing the backs of my knuckles, too, and she nods. I press my forehead to hers, squeezing my eyes shut. Fuck. This woman.

"I have condoms in the nightstand," she whispers, tilting her head toward the bedside table next to us. Then she bites her lower lip and says, "But it's been a while for me, and I just had my annual... I've got an IUD and I'm clean—"

Sweet Father Christmas, is she really saying what I think she's saying?

She shrugs then, staring up at me. The motion jostles her breasts where they're pressed against my chest. "I just mean, if you're... you know. Clean, too. If you want."

"I've never gone bare with anyone before, Noelle," I whisper, shifting my hips so that the head of my cock is lined up with that slick channel. "But I'd really like it if I could feel all of you."

She nods quickly, flattening my palm against her cheek and turning her face into it. I lift on my elbow slightly and she spreads her thighs wider, allowing me better access. The heat of her is scorching as I press just the tip inside. Tipping her face toward mine, I seal my lips over hers and work my hips, pushing the rest of the way in. Her mouth goes slack beneath my own and a breathy sigh of a moan leaves her when I bottom out, circling my hips against hers. *Holy hell*.

Nothing has ever felt so right. Being inside Noelle, feeling her tighten around me, her mouth under mine and those eyes laser focused on me... I'm done for. She can have all of me, everything I have. My body, my heart, my soul. Everything. It's all hers.

Shifting, I slide both arms beneath her body, holding her close against me as I begin to move. One of her hands finds purchase in my hair at the back of my head, urging my mouth back to hers while the other hand flattens at the small of my back. Her fingernails dig in and I chuckle. My little Angel is a bit of a hellcat.

Propping myself up on my forearms, I pull out and slam back in, her gasps getting lost in my kisses. Our hearts are pounding together where we're pressed so tightly against the other, and she wraps both arms around my neck, holding me close as I pound into her.

"So good, so fucking good," I rasp in time to our movements. "Goddamn, Noelle."

"Theo," she whimpers against my mouth, and that sound makes me a little insane.

Her pussy is squeezing me tight with each thrust that takes me all the way in, and it's not long before I feel the telltale tug in my balls that signals my impending release.

"I'm going to come," I warn, slowing my thrusts just a little. "Can you give me one more?"

I know she can, I can already feel those little fluttering spasms that tells me she's close again, too. She tosses her head on the bed as her legs begin to shake where they're clamped around my hips. "Don't stop, Theo. Right there. Please."

Shifting just a little, I slide my hand between our bodies and circle my thumb around her clit. She clenches around me and my mouth drops open. Oh shit. I work her harder, and then she's coming again, tightening around me like a vice.

"Ohmygod, ohmygod."

I can't help it then, my hips slam into hers over and over, hard enough that it makes the headboard bang against the wall above our heads, sending the lights strung up along it to rattle and dance in a colorful show across the wall. She continues to writhe beneath me, lost to her pleasure, and then I'm coming in long spurts, filling her. Stars burst at the corners of my vision as my orgasm wracks through me. I groan through it, my breath stuttering and my heart trying it's damndest to pound its way out of my chest.

Her hands splay wide over my ass, holding me tight against her as we come down together. I drag my mouth over her cheek, her throat, the curve of her shoulder.

"Holy shit," she whimpers, breathless and panting against the skin of my throat. Her lips flutter over the underside of my jaw. She's fucking perfect. "That was—"

I chuckle again when her words cut off on another soft moan. Pressing my mouth to hers, I whisper, "I know, Angel. For me, too."

Chapter Nineteen

Noelle

Theo untangles himself from me and I can't quite bite back the moan as he slides out of me. He grins, that boyish, mischievous grin I like the most, and leans back down to press a kiss to my mouth. "Stay put."

Like I'm going anywhere. My body feels like jell-o. I'm sure if I tried to stand, my knees would wobble like a newborn giraffe.

He stands then heads out of the bedroom, completely naked. I prop my head in my hand and watch him walk away. He's built like a basketball player; all long, lithe limbs and narrow hips, though his shoulders are wide, and every inch of him is trimmed in lean muscle. Now that I've seen Theo naked, I don't ever want him to put clothes back on or cover that body from my sight again.

He comes back a minute later with a wet washcloth and kneels on the bed. I stare up at him, one brow raised and unmoving, and he narrows his eyes at me. "Noelle..."

I roll my eyes, earning myself a deep growl from him, but I flop back onto my back and let him part my thighs. His touch is gentle as he cleans me up, and then he leans down and presses a kiss to the tip of one of my hipbones. I've always been tall and on the skinnier side, and until I was almost into my twenties, I'd been all knobby knees and gangly limbs.

I trail my fingers through his blonde locks as he skims his lips across my hip, and then his eyes find mine. The intensity in them is so potent... and I know what he's trying to say without actually saying the words out loud.

Now that I know its there, I'm a little surprised that I never realized it before. How could I have missed all of this for so long? His feelings are like a glowing neon sign blazing 'do you see me now?'. And I do. I see all of it. All of him.

Theo's been my best friend since we were six... and I had no idea this side of him existed.

The goofy, fun-loving Theo that I've known my entire life.

The sweet, kind Theo that is always at my side no matter what.

This dominant, sexy Theo? Totally new and its making me swoon, hard.

But this Theo, with the shutters pulled back and his full, undisputable feelings on display in those blue eyes... it's making me feel things I'd never even dreamed of.

My best friend has been... what? *In love with me?* For years?

This is some Hallmark Christmas movie level of rom-com craziness. And I'm totally here for all of it.

"Your skin is so soft here," he whispers, drawing his mouth across my body again. It sends shivers up my belly, and goosebumps flash across my skin. He chuckles, winking up at me. "So sensitive."

"You're mean," I grumble, narrowing my eyes at him.

He shifts on the bed and moves me so that I'm lying on my side, then slides one arm between my thighs so he can prop himself on his elbow across the leg that is flat against the bed, his arm curling around my other thigh so he can rest his cheek in his palm. My thigh is trapped in the cage of his arm, and from there he lowers his mouth to the top of my thigh where it meets my hip. I flinch, the brush of his lips tickling that sensitive spot. His other hand trails over the flat plane of my stomach and ribs, then back down to the lower part of my abdomen. That blue gaze follows his hand everywhere he touches, before raising to mine again.

"So, are you going to kick me out in the snow?" he asks quietly, still trailing his fingers over my stomach, back and forth. I smirk down at him. He glares at me and warns, "Just remember, Noelle, if you brat, I will punish you."

Biting my lip, I grin. "I do kind of like your version of punishments, Theo."

He nips my thigh and I gasp at the sharp sting, but then I laugh shakily. His voice is low and husky when he chuckles out, "Naughty thing."

"Always," I whisper-taunt. Sinking my fingers into his hair, I push the blonde strands away from his forehead. His head tilts against my fingers, as if he can't get enough of my touch, too. It makes me feel like the Grinch when his heart grows three sizes. "But to answer your question: no, I'm not kicking you out in the snow. I think I'd like it if you stayed with me tonight. Please."

"I wasn't going anywhere even if you said yes," he teases, winking up at me again. I roll my eyes and shake my head. A sharp pinch on my ass cheek elicits a startled yelp out of me and I laugh. He yawns broadly then, letting his cheek rest against the thigh he has his arm wrapped around. "I've been up since four-thirty this morning and you wore me out."

"One and done? We need to work on your stamina, old man," I taunt, stretching my arms over my head and elongating my body, putting it shamelessly on display for him. Those blue eyes darken and narrow on my face, and I smirk again, biting my lower lip. I love teasing Theo.

He releases my thigh and crawls up my body like a predatory cat; and I'm the prey. Stretching out beneath him, where he's bridged over me by his muscular arms and thighs, I giggle at the dark growl that rumbles out of his chest. His eyes leave my face and he grins then, reaching up and untwining the string of lights along my headboard. Oh shit.

"Turn over, Angel," he rasps, and I do as I'm told. Flat on my stomach, he manacles first one wrist, then the other, pulling them together above my head. He wraps my fingers around the metal bars of my headboard. The strand of lights is bound around my wrists and through the metal bars, anchoring my hands to the headboard, though that's all he binds this time. My cheek is pressed against the bedsheet and my breaths are coming out in short, shallow puffs of air. I can just see him over my shoulder out of my peripheral. Once he's satisfied my wrists are thoroughly bound, he sits back and then nudges my thighs apart so he can kneel between them. His hands drop to my ass, kneading it, spreading my cheeks. He groans, then his thumbs are trailing between my thighs, along the slickness there. "Fuck, so pretty. Are you ready? Naughty girls get fucked hard and fast, Noelle."

I nod, my cheek sliding against the coolness of the bedsheet beneath me. "Yes. Please."

I can feel the bed shift between my legs and then the blunt, broad head of his cock is there, pressing in. As he slides in, he moves so that he is leaning over my back, bridged above me by his arms on either side of my shoulders. This angle presses him in deep and he hits that spot that lights me up from the inside. Rolling my head, I press my forehead into the mattress and groan sharply at the pleasure, my fingers tightening around the cool metal my hands are anchored to. Holy fuck that feels amazing.

He lowers himself so that his chest is pressed against my back and his mouth grazes that spot where my neck and shoulder meet as he starts to move. Hard, fast, deep thrusts that take him so deep I'm not sure of anything other than I never want this to end. I've never been able to come from penetration by itself, but good god, I'm about to. I throw my head to one side, sucking deep, panting breaths in as my heart threatens to explode out of my chest. I clamp my fingers tight, my arms going taut above my head. Something tightens inside of me and suddenly I'm panicking, because—

"Oh god, Theo, stop," I cry, my arms straining against the bonds of the lights. "I'm going to... *Theo I have to pee!*—"

He chuckles darkly from behind me, his teeth grazing over my shoulder sharply, but he doesn't stop. I buck against him; he doesn't understand. Oh god, this is so embarrassing. I squeeze my eyes shut and fight the feeling. Oh god, oh god—

"Good girl. Don't fight it, Noelle." His words are barely audible through the whooshing in my ears. I start to shake uncontrollably. Ooooh god, it's happening—

"No, no no," I moan, and then my body explodes, coming so violently that I scream, and I bury my face in the mattress to muffle the sound and to hide my embarrassment as something gushes out of me. Theo pounds into me, harder than before and my body just keeps coming, my release tearing through me. I think I might be dead. "*Ohmygoooodd.*"

"Goddamn, such a good fucking girl," he groans out on a guttural growl. And then I feel him come, pulsing inside me as he empties deep into me. He presses his mouth against a spot directly between my shoulder blades, his chest heaving against my back as he shakes through his own orgasm. I've never come so hard in my life, little lights are dancing at the corners of my vision.

I can't catch my breath, and I'm so embarrassed I could cry. But then one of his hands is tipping my face toward his, and he seals his mouth over mine in a voracious kiss.

"I'm so sorry," I whisper, mortification burning my cheeks. I can feel the wetness beneath my hips, my thighs. I groan from the embarrassment.

"Sorry?" he asks, still catching his own breath. "For what? I'm so fucking proud of you."

"What?" I whisper breathlessly, still mortified, but now confused, too.

His brows pull together and he drags his mouth over mine again. "Angel, you just came so hard you squirted for me. You've never done that before?"

I shake my head. I didn't just pee? Oh thank fucking god.

Theo quickly unwinds the lights from around my wrists and pulls me up. I'm shaking from head to toe, and he gathers me into his arms, holding me tight against his chest. "You beautiful, wonderful thing. You're fucking perfect."

And then he wraps me in the comforter and sets me in the chair across the room with a tall glass of water as he strips the bed, lays down a few towels, then remakes the bed with clean sheets.

"Merry fucking Christmas to me," he chuckles as he leads me back to the bed, then climbs in beside me, pulling me close again. I laugh, shaking my head, but as soon as my cheek rests against Theo's chest, where I can hear his heart thudding a steady cadence, I'm asleep.

Chapter Twenty

Noelle

There was nothing in life that would have prepared me for waking up the next morning to the aftermath of sleeping with my best friend.

Theo and I have slept together too many times to count for it to be appropriate, honestly. Since we were kids, we've had sleepovers. Obviously they stopped for a time between middle school and graduating high school, but I can't count the times we've fallen asleep together on the couch, watching movies or whatever sports game was on TV. Study nights that went late. In our college years—and admittedly even after—we went home together after parties or late nights out at the bar and crashed in the same bed to sleep it off.

Not once has it ever been awkward... well, for me at least. He's always been my safe space, my rock. Even if we have always bickered like an old married couple and tormented each other mercilessly, he's just always been... *my Theo*. My best friend, my confidant. My person, I guess. Our friendship has always just been easy, and the occasional sleepover with him was just a normal thing. I thought so, anyway. Looking back on the numerous times it's happened over the years now, I'm sure if these feelings he's finally revealing go back as far as he says they do, things had to have been at least a little awkward for him.

But waking up, naked and sore and deliriously sated, next to an also naked Theo...yeah, I could get used to this. I'm laying facing him, one of his arms draped over my waist and our legs are tangled together like a pretzel. He's a furnace, and I'm a little shocked at how well I slept, because I'm fairly roasting now that I'm awake. And I have to pee.

The light filtering in through my bedroom window is muted and gray, which means it's either very early, or still snowing. I can only imagine the amount of snow piling up on his car, in my driveway... the roads are probably a hazard to be out on if it is in fact still snowing.

As carefully as I can, I manage to unwind myself from him and slip out of bed. Tiptoeing to the dresser, I pull the first long sleeved shirt I find out of the drawer and shove my head and arms into it. It's one of my dad's old shirts that I'd pilfered when Mom had finally gone through his things and decided what to get rid of, and it's far too big on me, so it hangs halfway down my thighs and the arms are about four inches too long.

It's a burgundy red, basic Glidden brand shirt with a pocket sewn into the left side and there's a hole in one of the armpits, but it's my favorite. It doesn't smell like him anymore, but sometimes I take it with me to Mom's and spray it with his cologne that I know she has tucked away in her bathroom.

I pluck a pair of tall socks out of the top drawer—Christmas themed fuzzy socks, Val would be so proud of me—and I hop on one foot, then the other, to shove my feet into them. Glancing over my shoulder at Theo, I ascertain that he's still sleeping soundly, then sneak out of the bedroom to the bathroom, then make my way out to the kitchen, where I start a large pot of coffee to brew.

Once it's ready, I pour myself a cup, spritz a little chocolate flavored whipped topping on it, then dust it with cinnamon. Walking over to the living room window, I look down at the crumpled, tangled mess of lights that Theo used to tie me up with last night, and my body burns all over again. Good lord the man's game is top tier.

Outside, the world is nothing but a blanket of white. Everything is covered in over a foot of snow, and even the street doesn't look like it's seen a snowplow yet. I glance at Theo's car; there's no way it's going to make it across town.

I bite my lower lip. Guess he's stuck here with me for a

little longer. I shiver with anticipation at the thought of being snowed in with Theo for who knows how long.

At the sound of my bedroom door swishing open, I turn, glancing over my shoulder as he emerges. He's in nothing but his black boxer briefs, his long, trim legs encased in the stretchy black fabric. His hips and waist are trim and narrow, his chest widening slightly. His shoulders are wide, lean muscle shifting as he reaches one arm up to scratch at the back of his neck as he walks toward me. He truly is beautiful.

He whistles long and low as he reaches me, his gaze traveling out the window along the snow-covered street. "I hope you have food in the fridge, I don't think we're getting out of here today."

I laugh, nodding as I turn back to the window. "Guess it's a good thing I went grocery shopping the other night, huh?" He steps up behind me, wrapping his arms around my shoulders, and rests his chin on the top of my head. I sigh, leaning back against his chest, careful not to spill my coffee still clutched between my palms. I press a kiss to the forearm that's crossed over my sternum. He shifts, lowering his head so he can graze his lips over the spot behind my right ear, and I can't help the smile that pulls at my mouth. My voice is barely a whisper as I say, "Good morning."

"Hmm," he murmurs low, squeezing me just a little tighter. "Merry Christmas."

I let my head fall to the side, leaning into his caress. God this feels so right. So natural. Like this is how it should have been all along. "Merry Christmas, Theo."

"Is there anymore coffee?" he asks, straightening. I give him a glare over my shoulder.

"No, I made just enough for myself."

He laughs as he walks around to the kitchen. "You really don't know how to not be a brat, do you?"

"Not when I'm awake," I counter, my tone sassy. He glares at me from beneath lowered brows as he pours himself a cup of coffee. I wink, and he shakes his head with a light scoff.

"Don't think being cute is going to get you out of trouble," he grumbles darkly, raising the mug to his lips. Those intense, baby blue eyes of his are fixed on me.

"Maybe I like being in trouble with you," I whisper. What I can only describe as a rumbly groan escapes him.

"You're going to be the death of my sanity," he grunts, shaking his head again. I grin over at him.

"Oh, how the tables have turned," I tease, making my way around the living room to the kitchen. I set my coffee on the counter then step in front of him. He glowers at me from over the rim of his cup as he takes another sip, then he sets it down with a thunk next to mine. Wrapping my arms around his naked torso, I lean into his chest as he wraps his arms around me as well. Turning my head, I plant a kiss to the very center of his chest. One of his hands buries itself in my hair at the back of my head, holding me to him. Spanning my hands wide across his back, I murmur directly against his skin, "How is it that this feels so right, Theo?"

The hand cupping the back of my head tightens in my hair so that he can tilt my face up toward his. His eyes, those beautiful blue eyes, search mine. "Because this is where we were always supposed to end up. It just took us a little while to get here."

My chest cracks open at his fervent, quiet words. "I wish you would have told me sooner."

His other hand cups my jaw and cheek in his palm, his thumb swiping over my bottom lip, his eyes just a little sad. "I was too scared to take the chance of telling you and having you pull away from me, Noe. I was selfish enough to need you in my life no matter how it needed to happen, just as long as I didn't lose you. I needed you too much, even if you never returned those feelings."

I take a deep breath, letting it out slowly. I don't know that

I return those same feelings that he has, not yet. I do know I love Theo, have always loved him. Just in a different way than he has... He hasn't come out and said the words, thankfully, because I'm not entirely sure I'm ready for that yet.

He smiles gently, swiping his fingers along my cheek and tucking my hair behind my ear. The gesture is sweet and so tender it makes my heart ache. "I know you know, and I know you well enough to know you're not ready for that, Angel. I won't say it yet, but I think we both know how I feel. All I ask is that you give this a chance, maybe let us see where it takes us. One day at a time. Please, Noelle."

My eyes bounce between his. God, he's so perfect. "One day at a time?"

Both of his hands frame my face, pushing my hair back over my shoulders and then he dips down to press his mouth to mine. It's a sweet, chaste kiss. Full of promise and beautiful opportunities.

"One day at a time," he repeats, his lips moving against my mouth.

I nod. One day at a time.

Chapter Twenty-One

Noelle

"What time is Belle supposed to be back?" Theo asks, staring out the window over the sink out into the still falling snow. At this rate, we'll be snowed in for days. Not that I mind.

"She isn't coming home until tomorrow, if this slows down at all and the plows can get out to clean up the roads."

My phone buzzes where its sitting on the end table, so I reach for it, swiping open the group chat that includes all three of us girls and Mom.

Mom

> Merry Christmas, girls! Noelle, did you and Theo get home okay last night?

Willow

> What are Val and I, chopped liver?

Val

> Val: *Eye roll emoji* You and Luck have
> like a two-minute drive home. Beau
> and I made it home safe, if anyone
> cares.

Mom

> Is there even one day where you girls
> don't bicker back and forth? Consider
> it my Christmas gift.

Me

> Your Christmas gift was letting you
> take over Beau's proposal. Yes, we
> made it last night. Theo crashed here
> so he didn't have to try and brave the
> roads again. Merry Christmas!

> And Val, congratulations again!

Willow

> Beside the point, Val. Guess we know
> who the favorite is.

Mom

> Willow Ann...

Val

> Thank you, Noe! You all did such a great job helping Beau plan! I was totally surprised! Is Theo still there because of the snow? Tell him we say Merry Christmas, too!

"Beau and Val say Merry Christmas," I call over to him.

"Merry Christmas, fam," he chuckles, shaking his head as he turns back toward the counter. I'm buried under a blanket on the couch. He's rifled through my cupboards, fridge, and freezer and found all the fixings to make homemade chicken pot pie soup. It's simmering currently, and smells divine. Theo also made homemade biscuits to go with it. The fluffy biscuits are cooling on a rack he found buried in one of the cabinets. My mouth is watering.

Me

> He says Merry Christmas, fam.

Mom

> Tell him to be careful if he decides to try and drive home today. Maybe he should just stay?

Me

Mom, are you trying to play match-maker?

Willow

Ha. Can you imagine? You and Theo? All you two do is fight.

Me

And? Your point?

Val

I think they'd be great together.

Willow

GIF of Lloyd Christmas gagging.

Mom

You know, Willow, one of these days Karma is going to bite you in the ass.

Willow

GIF of Police K-9 biting a man in the rear

> **Bring it on. I'll have treats in my pocket just in case.**

> **You're all ridiculous. Get a life. Merry Christmas. We're going to eat and watch Tim Allen's 'The Santa Clause'.**

I click my phone off and shake my head. What are they going to say when they find out about, well, whatever this is between me and Theo? What are we going to tell them?

Theo is giving the chicken pot pie soup another stir before he replaces the lid, then brushes his hands off. He's dressed in the same shirt and jeans he was wearing yesterday. "This needs to simmer for a bit longer and then it will be ready. Do you want to open your present now? I can go grab it from the car."

I haul my butt out of the corner of the couch, letting the blanket fall. "I'll come out with you. I should shovel a pathway at least."

"You can stay in here," he says, coming to me and wrapping his arms around my waist. "I'll only be just a second."

"It's okay, I'll come out with you."

"That obsessed with me, huh?" he teases, pecking my lips twice before lingering and deepening the kiss.

"Like I said, you're so cocky," I laugh, leaning away,

though I keep my arms looped around his shoulders. My fingers brush through the blonde locks at the back of his head.

"We're just getting started, Angel," he breathes against my lips.

I shove at his chest, laughing again. "I need to go put on some pants."

He lets both hands slide down my body and beneath the hem of the oversized shirt I'm wearing to cup both bare ass cheeks. "I like you with no pants on."

I arch one brow at him, smirking. "Yeah? Should we give the neighbors a show?"

He slaps one palm against my ass and I gasp in shock. He growls low at me as he nips my shoulder. "No one gets to see this perfect fucking body but me, Noe. Every glorious inch of you is for my eyes only."

I nod weakly, my bottom lip caught between my teeth as his own teeth graze the flesh of my throat. "Okay."

He gives my ass another slap, then pushes me away. "You have three minutes or I'm going out on my own."

I hightail it into the bedroom, pulling on a pair of sweats, and then I'm back. He's already got his boots on as well as the gray quilted vest zipped up his chest. I shove my feet into my boots, pull my jacket, gloves, and my favorite winter hat with a pompom on the crown of it, and we're out the door.

I go to grab the shovel by the door, but he beats me to it. Theo makes quick work of the little porch that has snow drifted up onto it, and then effortlessly clears a pathway to his car. He hands the shovel back to me with a smirk, then reaches into the backseat for the bag of gifts we'd unwrapped the night before. Walking back to the porch, he's almost to the door when I fling myself into the completely undisturbed snow in the front yard, flat on my back. I swish my arms and legs out, carving out a snow angel, before remaining where I am. The snow has slowed just the slightest, but it's still coming down in fat flakes. I open my mouth, sticking out my tongue, and do my best to catch some of them as they fall on my face. The sky above me is white from the clouds and snow.

A muffled thump and then puff of snow flutters at me and I turn my head to the side, grinning, as Theo stretches out in the snow next to me. He does the same thing, moving his arms and legs around to make his own snow angel, and then he turns to look at me. His hand stretches out to mine and I set my mittened hand in his, just our fingers barely touching.

"You asked me the other night what I wanted for Christmas. And I said that Santa couldn't bring me what I wanted," he says softly, his blue eyes searching mine intensely. "This,

Noelle. All I've wanted for so long, is this. With you. My best friend."

I nod, my head moving against the snow squished beneath me. "I'm glad Santa was able to come through for you, Theo."

He shifts, moving closer—and ruining both our beautiful snow angels—until he's propped up on one elbow directly beside me. His other hand slides against my now cold cheek, and his fingers are chilled, too. And then he leans down and kisses me, thoroughly, unhurriedly, like we have all the rest of our days to do so, right in the middle of my front yard for anyone to see.

Chapter Twenty-Two

Theo

We're both chilled and wet from the snow by the time I stand and pull her up with me. We walk, hand in hand, back to the front door. We strip out of our winter gear, hanging it up to dry, before making our way to the bedroom and shucking off our pants that are wet and cold. She digs around in her closet, on the hunt for something that might fit me.

She pulls her dad's shirt that she's still wearing off and hands it to me, it's the only shirt she has that will fit me, then she shrieks 'Aha!' when she locates a pair of my sweatpants I'd left here ages ago in the back of her closet.

I pull them on while she puts on some Christmas themed pajamas—because, of course she does—and then she's dragging me back out into the kitchen. I put her to work building us a couple Peppermint Schnapps hot chocolates as I dish up the pot pie soup.

"Your nose is pink." My heart is happy, being here with

her like this. It's all I've ever wanted, and I'm still waiting for someone to come and steal her away, or for her to run from me. Like this somehow isn't real, or won't stay. Leaning down to her, I rub the tip of my nose against hers in an Eskimo kiss, which earns me one of those full, uninhibited Noelle smiles that sends my heart to galloping in my chest. Goddamn she's so fucking beautiful.

Earlier, after I'd rolled out the biscuits and cleaned off the counter, she'd hopped up to sit on the counter in front of me. It was easy to see what she wanted, she's as easy to read as an open book, and it had been my pleasure to give it to her.

Laying her down on the counter before me, I'd barely lowered my jeans to free my rock-hard cock before sliding inside her, all the way to the hilt. Her back had arched off the counter as I went deep, her hands sliding beneath her shirt to play with her nipples as I'd thrust hard and deep and long. Watching her come apart beneath me, feeling her come around my cock buried so fucking deep... it's all I want to do for the rest of my days. I want every fucking part of her. Her sass, her sadness, her joy, her pleasure... her heart and her soul. I want all of it.

I had bitten back the words that keep trying to fall off my tongue every fucking time I look at her. Instead, I'd pounded into her, hard, powerful thrusts while my fingers dug into her hips that had her screaming through the orgasm that tore through her minutes later. My own orgasm is curling around my spine, tightening my balls, and making my chest seize. Slamming my palm against the countertop, I come, filling her in long, hot spurts.

We laughed through cleaning up our mess, our hands and lips finding each other constantly, as if neither one of us can stand to be apart. Like she needs me just as much as I need her.

Now, I carry our soups and the platter of biscuits to the coffee table in front of the couch while she finishes topping our hot chocolates. I press play on the movie queued up on the TV, then sink into my usual corner of the couch, dragging the blanket up as I settle on the couch. Noelle folds her legs beneath her criss-cross style as she settles directly against my side. Another heart stopping change that I'm going to have to get used to, instead of having her across the couch from me, and I drape the blanket over our laps before handing over her food.

Our legs are sandwiched together beneath the blanket, our arms pressed against the other as we sit side by side and eat. She groans around a mouthful of the savory soup. "This is amazing, Theo."

"I'm glad you like it," I chuckled before taking another bite myself. "It's one of the few things I can make."

"Well, one of us is going to have to learn how to cook if we're going to make this a thing," she teases, bumping her shoulder into mine lightly. My chest cracks open at her words. Such possibility in that little statement. That possibility of a future, that—just maybe—she might want that with me, too. I try not to put too much stock into what she said, but damn, it's hard not to when it's all I've wanted. "Otherwise, we'll both starve."

"I think we'll be able to figure it out," I tease back gruffly, my throat tight. "One day at a time, right?"

She smiles up at me, nodding, and then she leans over and presses a kiss to the tip of my shoulder. It's sweet and tender and comfortable, like we've been doing this for forever. This is how it's supposed to be. "One day at a time, Theo."

I take another bite of the soup, singeing my mouth on the still scorching hot liquid. This woman is going to be the death of me.

By the time she's finished her first bowl of soup, I've polished off two and a handful of the flakey, buttery biscuits. The woman doesn't know how to pour a light drink, and the peppermint schnapps in the hot chocolate is strong. I throw one arm across her shoulders as she sets her bowl next to mine on the coffee table and pull her into my side. I press a kiss to the top of her head, breathing her in.

"Can I give you my present, now?" I ask against her hair.

"Sure," she says, shifting sideways as I push to my feet.

I pluck the still gift-wrapped present from the bag that I'd left by the door and hand it to her before sitting back down. My heart is beating a hundred miles a minute.

She tears at the paper, tossing it to the floor in a heap, before turning over the framed picture. I hold my breath.

It's a matte framed photo of the night sky, hundreds of stars and a sliver of the moon in the navy background. She looks up at me, her brows furrowing over those green eyes in confusion. I swallow hard. Here goes nothing, I guess.

"The other night, when I asked you what you wanted for Christmas, you said, very sarcastically, might I add, 'the moon and all the stars'…"

Her mouth drops open in awe, her gaze sliding back to the photo in her lap.

"This is the night sky from the very first day we met," I murmur quietly, my throat tight.

"Like, from the first day of *kindergarten*?" she asks, looking up at me. Her green eyes are shimmering. I nod, reaching up to brush my knuckles across her cheek.

"If I'm going to give you the moon and all the stars, I figure it should be from the very first day I fell in love with you, Noelle."

"Oh," she breathes and I watch as tears line her lower lids. "Theo..."

"I know I said I wouldn't say it yet, but I can't not say this to you, Angel," I whisper, leaning in to press my forehead against hers. "You don't have to say it back. I just need you to know how I feel. How I've always felt, Noe."

"Theo," she whispers again, but this time it makes my heart stutter. It's hesitant, guarded. *Fuck*. "This is a lot more than taking it one day at a time..." She shifts next to me, so that she can face me more fully. I can't bring myself to meet her eyes, to see the rejection there. Fucking hell. I should have known better. She clasps my face between her hands and tugs my face up, forcing me to look at her. "Theo. You know I love you. You've been my very best friend for so long. You're my person," she whispers earnestly, pressing her forehead to mine this time. "This is a lot to take in all at once."

I nod. Fuck. I know it is. But it's like this dam has broken inside of me, and I've waited decades to let it all out. Now, there's no slowing the outpouring. "I just needed you to know, Noelle. Fuck... I just don't want to lose you now that you know—"

She shakes her head, her lips dragging over mine, stopping the flow of words.

"You're not going to lose me," she breathes against my lips. "I don't want to lose you, either, Theo. You're my person. Always."

"One day at a time," I whisper. "We can do that."

"One day at a time," she repeats, nodding again. It's the best Christmas gift I could have asked for. The possibility of a future with Noelle.

Epilogue
Noelle

One Year Later

Theo drags me by the hand down the semi darkened hallway of my mom's house, away from the rest of our family where they're congregated in the kitchen for our Compton's/Collins Christmas Chaos, going absolutely gaga over the ultrasound pictures that Val and Beau had surprised Mom, Marnie, and Drew with. I've already seen them, having gone with her to the appointment several weeks ago. Beau hadn't even known until after the OB appointment, as Val hadn't wanted to get his hopes up if it was false. The man had gone absolutely bananas over the little kidney bean shaped baby that was just barely a blip at the time of the ultrasound.

Theo stops, turning toward me with a devilish grin on his lips. I have a half a second to admire how just ridiculously handsome my boyfriend is before he's pushing me up against the wall at the end of the hallway, in the shadows. Our hands are frantic and all over each other. It's been a year, and I still can't get enough of him.

We did the whole 'one day at a time' thing for all of about two weeks before I couldn't *not* say those three little words back to him. And the rest had been history. Who couldn't fall head over heels for Theo? The man is... good god he's just incredible. Sweet and kind and funny and so fucking good in bed it's honestly not fair.

Our families had been over the moon when we'd finally let them all in on the secret. Mom and Marnie had looked at each other and said something like 'Called it' and Beau had clapped Theo on the back, telling him he was so proud that his balls had finally dropped enough to make a move on me.

Now, he brackets my face with his hands, those long, talented fingers spanning wide so that he can tip my face up toward his. Leaning into me, he grinds his hips against my middle and I moan, rocking my own body into the hardness there. That stupid fucking Santa hat is on his head again, though I secretly love it.

"Our parents are going to come searching for us," I whisper between kisses, and he shakes his head.

"Not likely," he grunts back, sinking his tongue into my mouth to kiss me fiercely, hungrily. He's unhinged and I love it. "They'll be swooning over that ultrasound for at least the next half an hour."

"Theo—" I groan breathily as he shoves his hand up my shirt, palming my breast through my bra. "Oh god. Do you think we could—"

He chuckles darkly, nipping my lower lip sharply, making me gasp. "You insatiable hussy. I'm not fucking you in an open hallway during family Christmas."

I whine, pouting. "Cock tease."

Theo grips my chin between his finger and thumb, forcing my head up so I have to meet his eyes. "Don't brat right now, Angel. Or you won't get your present."

"If my present isn't your cock shoved down my throat or in my pussy, I'm not interested," I grumble around another groan, the fingers of his other hand pinching my nipple hard. He laughs out loud, dropping his forehead to mine.

"You're impossible," he laughs, shaking his head. Raising his hand, he forces my chin up higher, until I'm forced to look straight up. My mouth drops open. Is that...?

"I plan to meet you under the mistletoe every year for the rest of my life," he whispers, lowering my chin so that I can look at him again.

Wrapping my arms around his neck, I pull his mouth

down to mine. We kiss and kiss until we're both breathless, and when he finally pulls away, I'm panting, trying to catch my breath, when he shocks me even further by sinking down onto one knee.

He pulls a small box out of his pocket and flips it open, turning it so I can see the dark stone that glistens like a million stars are captured inside it. It's stunning, surrounded by tiny white diamonds.

"Take this life one day at time with me, Noelle. For forever. Waiting for you was one of the hardest things I ever had to do... but I'd have waited forever for you, Noelle. I love you and I always have. There will never be a day where you don't consume every part of me," he murmurs, his voice thick with emotion. I can't help it, I sink down to the floor in front of him, kneeling before him and taking his face in my hands. This amazing, handsome, perfect man that loves me. "Please, Noelle. Marry me."

"That wasn't a question," I laugh brokenly, tears choking me as they slide down my cheeks.

"It's not a question," he answers, turning to press his lips to one of my palms. "You're too much of a brat to get the option to say no."

"Well, if I don't have any other option..." I whisper, pursing my lips as if thinking about it. Like my answer isn't an irrefutable yes. "You just had to copy Beau, huh?"

"*Noelle...*" he warns, that deep, low growl rumbling out of his chest making me shiver. Oh, I'll be in so much trouble later for this. I grin widely, spanning my fingers over his jaw on either side. I rub my thumb over his bottom lip and he nips it sharply, those blue eyes laser focused on mine.

"Oh, for the love of— *Would you just say yes already?*" my sister's shrill voice echoes down the hall and we both laugh, turning to look where just her head is popped out from around the wall by the living room. I blush furiously. How long has my sister been eavesdropping, and how much of that did she hear? Are they *all* listening to this? Theo's awkward laugh tells me he's wondering the same thing.

"Yes!" I shout down the hall, making our families whoop and cheer from where they were clearly all listening in. Then, turning to the amazing man in front of me, I whisper for only him to hear, "Yes, my love. I will marry you and take this life one day at a time with you. I love you, Theo Collins."

I don't even get the words all the way out before he's hauling me into his arms, crushing me to his chest, his mouth crashing down onto mine. The ring box clatters to the floor, but neither of us care. Because it's not about the ring. This is about us.

I grin against his mouth. This is quite possibly the best Christmas ever.

Lucky in Love

Want to know Willow and Luck's beginning?
Coming March 2025!
Featuring Willow Compton and Reeve Luck in an
enemies-to-lovers, feuding neighbors, drunken bet, spicy romance!

*NOTE that these novellas are published SLIGHTLY out
of order due to time constraints on my end.
When the full series is completed (by the end of 2025) they can
be read in order by holiday in a calendar year!
The reading order will be as follows:
Be Mine, Valentine
Lucky In Love
Birthday Wishes
Halloween Night
Meet Me Under the Mistletoe
Midnight Kiss

Acknowledgements

I truly cannot believe that we are here at the end of my seventh book already, and number three in the Holiday Novella Collection! What an adventure this has been, and I truly feel so blessed to be doing what I love! Thank you all for your continued love and support throughout this journey!

Mom, you were my first and always my biggest fan, and the best proofreader around. Without your love and support this wouldn't have been possible! You knew when I was fifteen that I would be here one day, even when I doubted it myself. On to book seven and eight (holy crap!) already with so many others on the way! I love you!

Nick my love, thank you for letting me hide away at my desk for hours—and sometimes days—on end. Thank you for messaging me that my breakfast, lunch, or dinner was waiting for me when I was ready for it, because you knew I wouldn't even think about eating (thank you, Chef). Thank you for your support, faith, and enthusiasm for this passion of mine. Without you and the love you give me, I wouldn't have started writing again. Without your support, I wouldn't be able to do this full-time. You are my favorite cheerleader, my love. You are my forever Prince Charming. I love you!

Kara, you have been such a champion in my corner, for your unwavering faith in these stories and in me! And THANK YOU for excitedly and willingly volunteering as tribute to come with me to all our author events! I can't wait to see what kind of trouble we can get into! Thank you for being one of the best friends a girl could ask for! And now for being my formatter extraordinaire! It looks amazing!

Melody with Aurora Publicity, thank you sooo much for the absolutely gorgeous cover!

To all my favorite author friendly Facebook groups: THANK YOU for allowing me to be unapologetic in my shameless promotions and all of you that have recommended The Petoskey Stone Series and this Holiday Romance Collection to this absolutely voracious world of spicy romance readers!

To my amazing Street Team and ARC Team, THANK YOU for loving these crazy characters and their stories as much as I do! I hope you all love Noelle and Theo as much as I do! I love all of you! So many of you that enthusiastically beta read, ARC read, and shout about these books from the rooftops, thank you!

To all the people that are not named but have beta read, listened to me venting or joined in my excitement over each new milestone, and all those that have rooted for me in this scary and enthralling journey, thank you! I wouldn't be here without you!

Lastly, to all my readers, old and new, this has only been possible because of the love and support you've shown me and these characters. I hope you love reading their story as much as I've loved writing it. Noelle and Theo are so fun and spicy, and I can't wait to give you Willow's story next! Thank you!

Meet the Author!

Danielle Baker, romance author of the Petoskey Stone Series and the Holiday Romance Novella Collection, was born and raised in the beautiful city of Petoskey, nestled on the crystalline shores of Lake Michigan. She is married to the love of her life, Nicholas, and they have four children between them. Danielle's love of writing began while she was in high school. She wrote a slew of short stories and had written three novels by the time she graduated. Life got busy and writing was put on hold for many years while she started her family. At the urging of her mother, sister, and husband, Danielle was given the boost she needed to "get back in the saddle" and keep reaching for her lifelong dream of becoming a published author. When Danielle isn't working, writing, or spending time with her family, she can be found with a cup of coffee in one hand and a book in the other.

www.ingramcontent.com/pod-product-compliance
Ingram Content Group UK Ltd.
Pitfield, Milton Keynes, MK11 3LW, UK
UKHW021503270825
7605UKWH00018B/202